Luke's Fate

By Kathleen Ball

Contemporary Western Romance

Copyright © 2016 by Kathleen Ball

All rights reserved. No part of this book may be used or reproduced in any form or by any means electronic or mechanical, including photocopying, recording or by any information storage and retrieval systems, without prior written permission of the author except where permitted by law.

Published by Kathleen Ball
Edited by Kay Springsteen Tate
Cover art by Ari Tan

The characters and events portrayed in this book are fictitious. Any similarity to real persons, living or dead, is coincidental and not intended by the author.

Dedication

I dedicate this book to Merriedth Province and to Bruce, Steven, Colt and Clara because I love them.

Chapter One

Meg O'Brien slowed her quarter horse, Merry. Her smile quickly turned into a frown as she spotted the ranch hands huddled together. Puzzled, she spurred Merry on to the barn, slid out of her saddle, and hurried toward the men.

They glanced at her and nodded but each briskly turned away. Unusual for them; she'd never had a problem with any of the hands since she started running the ranch.

"What's going on?"

They shuffled their feet and kept their gazes on the ground.

She stared at the youngest hand, Ron. He was about seventeen, near as she could tell, and scrawny with dark hair and eyes. He'd spill the beans. He seemed to sense that he was in her sites, and he glanced up. His eyes widened before he looked away.

"Ron, what's going on around here?"

Ron tipped his sweat-stained Stetson at her and smiled. "We have ourselves a guest."

Running out of patience, she touched Greg's arm. He'd been her right hand from the start. His blue eyes searched hers. He had a nasty scar on his face, but she hardly noticed it anymore. "Tell me."

"Kelly's here. He's in the bunkhouse."

Her heart beat faster, and a lump grew in her throat. "Luke Kelly?"

Greg nodded and gave her a sympathetic smile.

Taking a deep breath, Meg turned toward the weathered bunkhouse, took two steps and stopped. Why was he here? She'd banked on never seeing him again.

For five years, she'd avoided serious relationships, and she didn't need Luke now. The back of her throat ached, and she swallowed hard. It was foolish to think he was back for her. He had no interest in her, because if he had, he would have never left.

She walked on, hardening her heart. She was the foreman, and that saddle bum was not going to hang his hat in her bunkhouse. Who did he think he was anyway?

The door creaked loudly as she opened it.

"Dad, what's going on?" Her dad had always been her rock, but age and a heart attack had slowed him down. It had taken a lot to persuade him to make her foreman, but she had prevailed.

"Luke is going to stay with us for a while."

She didn't like the worry reflected in his weary eyes. Slowly, she turned to where Luke sat and suppressed a gasp. Her big, hunky hero was a ghost of his former self, and the gauntness of his face was just the beginning. His blue eyes lacked emotion. He hadn't shaved, and his dark beard was long and unkempt. His usual tight fitting clothes hung on him.

"Luke?" she whispered.

He glanced at her, gave her a semblance of a smile, and then turned away.

"Dad?"

"Luke has run into some hard times, and I offered to let him stay here."

The air seemed to grow heavy and it became difficult to breathe, and her stomach churned. She couldn't see him every day, she just couldn't. "Stay here?"

"Yes, honey, for as long as he needs."

She felt for Luke, but he couldn't stay. She'd lose her sanity and her heart for sure if he remained.

Meg stepped outside for some fresh air and sat on the top step of the wrap around porch, staring at the bunkhouse. Nerves had her clasping and unclasping her hands. She needed her father to come out and explain. What the hell had happened to Luke? She couldn't remember seeing anyone look so bad. He appeared lost and, oh God, maybe he was sick or dying. That would explain his gauntness. Of course, he'd want to come home.

Well, as close to home as he could get. His dad had sold her father the land, he'd sold the house to a young family with a slew of kids, and then he had moved into a retirement home not too far away. Did Harry Kelly even know his boy was home?

Her father slowly ambled across the yard. She couldn't wait so she stood and ran to him. "Dad, is he sick? Is he dying?"

"Whoa, Margaret Mary, he'll heal eventually."

"What are you talking about?"

He took her hand and led her to the porch. "Here sit. Luke has had a hard time of it lately, and he came here to get his head straight."

"The truth, Dad, Luke looks like he's been through hell and back."

She sat on the edge of the old wooden chair, and her father gave her a sad smile. "He has, and it's up to us to give him room to regain himself."

"You're not going to tell me, are you?" Meg stood, put her hands on her hips, and stared at her father.

"Honey, it's not my story to tell. Besides, I gave him my word."

"Well, I guess that's it, then." A man's word was a powerful thing.

He smiled. "I knew you'd understand. Now, could you make him something to eat? Something light on the stomach?"

Meg pulled the screen door open. "Sure, Dad."

She headed into the big kitchen and pulled out all the ingredients to make beef soup. She worked quickly, trying to keep her mind focused on the soup, but all she could think about was the last time she'd seen Luke. He'd taken her dancing, and it was such a magical time. At the end of the night, he had walked her to the door, kissed her goodnight, and held her as though he didn't want to leave. It was only a few kisses actually, and foolishly, she'd thought he felt something for her. She'd been in love with him since forever but never had the nerve to let it show.

She went to bed that night thinking they were starting a relationship. She'd been so happy and full of dreams. Senseless dreams, she reminded herself. She shook her head at her stupidity.

The next day she waited for him to call or drop over. Her heart ached as the hours went by. A few days later, she went to town to see some friends and she heard that Luke had left town. He'd left right after their date. To her shame, she cried in front of her friends and became an object of ridicule and pity.

Never again. She'd never allow her heart to be ripped out like that again, and she'd never show her feelings to anyone. It was easier to be alone.

The soup was ready, and she ladled some into a bowl. A shiver raced through her at the thought of bringing it to him. Gathering her courage, she headed toward the bunkhouse.

But when she got there, he was sound asleep. Meg put the soup and bread on the old wooden table in the dining area and watched Luke sleep. His breathing seemed erratic to her, causing concern. Her gaze traveled his body. Just as she thought, he'd lost most of his bulk. Sighing, she wondered what happened. He used to be into fitness.

Her father said that Luke would heal. Maybe he'd been in some sort of accident. Could be a horse threw him. She didn't understand the getting his head on straight part. Her heart cried out to sit on the side of the bunk and caress his thin face. Even with his awful beard, she wanted to touch him.

Her stomach coiled in sudden need, and she jolted back to reality. There would be no touching, ever.

Luke stirred and opened his weary eyes. His eyes widened, filled with warmth, and then all emotion faded. The light faded from his eyes. "Looking good, Margaret Mary. Your eyes are still the bluest, and your hair is still the same sable color. It's nice to know some things never change."

She blinked hard at the gruffness of his voice. "Do you want to get up to eat or do you want to eat in your bunk?"

"I'll get up."

He struggled to sit, and when he swung his feet to the floor he swayed as though he was going to faint. As he started to rise, she raced to his side putting her arm around his waist. The jolt of emotion that flew through her made her cringe. He still had it, the ability to make her forget herself.

"Thanks." He gave her a weak smile.

It wasn't easy, but she helped him to the table and sat him in a chair. Whatever had happened was his own doing, she reminded herself. He was the one who had left.

"The soup is good, Marg—"

"Meg...you know my name is Meg."

"Still easy to rile, Meg. I'm glad I'm here."

"Well, if you don't need me for anything else, I have a ranch to run."

"You've changed. You used to smile all the time. I've yet to see one."

"You're right, I have changed. I'll send Ron in to help you get back to bed." Before he could reply, she fled. Resting her back against the outside of the barn, she took a deep breath. She'd wanted to scream at him and tell him he was the reason she didn't smile, but she had her pride.

Men weren't necessities. Not for her. As long as he stayed out of her way… Oh hell, who was she kidding? He was as helpless as a motherless calf. It galled her that she'd end up being the mother. Mother would be better than girlfriend or wife. A mother wouldn't have the longings she had for that man.

She had a ranch to run anyway. She didn't have time for love or for Luke. The ranch hands could help him back on his feet.

But why wouldn't her heart forget him? The dull ache she felt daily was now a sharp, throbbing pain.

Luke sighed as he watched Meg leave, and regret instantly filled his heart. She was lovely. He'd thought about her, more often than not, the last five years. His father had a loathing for all things O'Brien, and he knew he was playing with fire when he'd asked her for a date. He'd known there would be consequences.

"Consequences be damned," he mumbled as he shoved the bowl of soup away.

So much had changed. His father had sold the ranch, but that wasn't such a surprise. The surprise was he sold it to the O'Briens. The irony of the situation wasn't lost on Luke. He shuddered. He was damned, all right.

His biggest regret was Meg's lost smile. He'd done that to her. Unfortunately, he wouldn't get a chance to make her smile. He needed to leave as soon as he was able.

"I've heard about you." Ron walked into the bunkhouse, sat at the beat up table and stared at him.

"No surprise there."

"Were you really the best mustang trainer around?"

He glared at Ron's eager face and nodded. "I was. A long time ago."

"What happened? Why'd you leave? Hell, Miss Meg won't even let me near your mustangs, and they're some beauts."

Luke's body stiffened, his mind whirled, and his heart beat faster. "My mustangs are here?"

"Sure are!"

He closed his eyes, letting out a deep breath. He'd been worried about those horses. He figured his father had gotten rid of them. A slight smile played across his lips. His Meg had them.

"Miss Meg is the foreman now?"

Ron turned red and nodded.

"I sure am the foreman." Meg stood in the doorway with her hands on her hips.

Ron grinned as he stared at her.

"Ron, I need you to go check on the new foals, watch them for a bit and make sure they're feeding."

"Yes, ma'am." Ron almost tripped over his feet in his excitement to do Meg's bidding.

"Nice kid." Luke took a moment to admire Meg. She'd filled out in all the right places. The only bit of femininity she had was her long, brown hair; otherwise, she dressed like the other cowboys. She appeared hard and cold. She probably had to be to keep the men in line, but it didn't suit her. He remembered pink was her favorite color, and her shirts were usually adorned with some type of flower. Now she was colorless.

"Yes, he's a good worker." Her gaze wandered, coming to rest on everything in the bunkhouse except him.

"He told me about the mustangs, Meg. I know you have them."

She shrugged her shoulders. "I bought them after you—well, after you left."

Her sadness enveloped him. What could he say to make things better? "Meg, I'm—"

She turned toward him and put her hand up with her palm facing him. "Stop, I don't want to hear anymore. I don't care why you left. Let's just leave it at that. Greg will be in to help you clean up a bit."

Once again, he watched her leave, and he frowned. Her walk was different, and her hips didn't sway anymore. That sway used to... There was no sense in thinking how things used to be.

Luke pushed away from the table, each muscle groaned in protest. He was stronger than before but still as helpless as a kitten. If Meg thought he was bad off now, she should have seen him... It was better this way. Funny how their roles had reversed, he'd been the strong one, and she'd been the sweetest little gal.

He shuffled his feet until he got to his bunk, and a moan escaped as he lowered himself down. Vertigo got to him, and he swayed slightly before he lay back. Tomorrow would be a good day to try to make it outside. The need to feel the wind on his face grew stronger every day.

He covered his eyes with his forearm. What did Meg see when she looked at him? Probably a man to be pitied, and she didn't even know the whole story. He'd been right to ask her dad, Owen, not to discuss his situation.

He shifted on the bunk, his moan echoed through the bunkhouse. *My body is stronger than yesterday and the day before.* It was a constant litany to get him through the day. He'd heal, at least his body would. It was the loved ones who'd died in the car crash that haunted him. He shuddered and a lone tear trailed down his face. The weight of the world was on his shoulders, a weight he deserved to bear.

Choices had ramifications, and it was something he'd always known, but not to the extent where lives changed irrevocably. Sure accidents happened and the one that killed his wife, Mary and his daughter, Jill was like many others. It was raining in Texas and the roads were slick. He was taking Mary and Jill to the ballet. They'd been so excited to see The Nutcracker. Luke smiled at the memory. His girls had worn matching red dresses for the occasion.

"Earth to, Luke."

He jumped at the sound of Ron's voice. "You startled me."

"Heck, I've been here for a minute or two jawing at you before I noticed you weren't listening to me." Ron laughed. "Miss Meg had me bring you some dinner."

Luke closed his eyes trying to put the past away. "That was good of you. Don't you and Greg eat here too?"

"Heck no, we eat at the house. Greg and me are batching it. The others all have homes to go to."

"I bet the O'Briens had to hire more men to work both spreads."

Ron nodded. "Here, let me help you to the table." He put his arm around Luke's back and helped him up.

Dizziness caused Luke to sway.

"Look man, I can bring the food to you."

"No, the more I get around the better. I just get dizzy at times, is all."

"To tell you the truth, you look like you got the wrong end of a bucking bull."

"I'm getting better and better. I plan to be able to go see my mustangs by the end of the week." Luke glanced up and spotted Meg leaning against the doorframe.

"They're my mustangs now. Just remember that." She spun on her boot heel and walked out the door.

"She sure is pretty when she's all riled up," Ron commented.

Luke shook his head. She had spirit, and whether she knew it or not, she'd just thrown down a challenge. He was going to ride his mustangs again, and he wasn't leaving until he did.

Damn! Ever since she told him that this was a working ranch, Luke was everywhere. A week ago, she'd waltzed into the bunk house and shoved a broom in his hand, telling him to earn his keep. At least she'd gotten a startled reaction from him. There was actually a bit of fire in his blue eyes as he took the broom from her.

Meg sighed and turned back to Merry. The love she had for her horse was deep. Besides her father, her love only went to her animals. She'd hardened the last few years, and now she didn't know any other way to be.

After she thrust the broom at Luke, she left the bunkhouse horrified by her actions. She'd never been cruel before. Now it appeared that she had done him a favor. Dad had said Luke was healing quickly, and his strength was coming back.

Glancing his way, she bristled as he smiled and waved. What was she going to do with him? He leaned against the ancient, wooden wall of the bunkhouse with his brown Stetson lowered over his eyes. His face was smooth; he really must be getting better if he'd found the strength to shave.

Her heart thumped, not from love, surely not from love. It was probably from fear. Meg turned back and finished saddling Merry. She didn't allow fear in her life, no it must be thumping due to worry or something.

The familiar creak of leather as she got into the saddle soothed her. Turning Merry, she lit out. It was a glorious day, and as soon as she figured she was far enough away to be out of Luke's sight, she took off her hat and unbound her hair, letting it fly free in the Texas breeze. She could be herself when she was away from everyone.

There would be no more heart thumping. She needed to confront her problems, and right now, her problem was Luke Kelly. According to her father, Luke was staying a good long time. She'd have to see about that. There had to be a way to encourage him to leave for good. Her whole routine had been turned upside down. The worst part was he was able to come to the house for dinner.

She'd nearly choked when he had shown up last night. Maybe it was time for Ron and Greg to eat in the bunkhouse with Luke.

She slowed Merry to a stop, rebraided her hair and put her hat back on. She smiled. That certainly would solve part of her problem. She'd tell them tonight. Relief washed through her as she rode home. A good plan of action always calmed her.

Her smile grew wider. Luke wasn't anywhere to be seen as she rode into the yard.

"Did you have a good ride?" Ron stared up at her with an odd grin on his face. He turned red when she nodded.

"Yes, I did thanks." She slid out of the saddle and started to lead Merry into the barn.

"Let me do that," Ron offered. "I just cleaned out the stalls."

"Thanks, Ron. I do need to talk to Dad."

Ron led Merry into the barn, and Meg walked to the house. The porch had been nicely swept, and she wanted to laugh, but she had matters to discuss with her father.

She found him in his office looking over some paperwork. His eyes crinkled into a smile when he spotted her.

"What brings you here? I hardly see my daughter anymore. I only see the foreman."

Meg furrowed her brow. "What does that mean?"

"Oh, Margaret Mary, don't get all hepped up. I just meant you look relaxed, not all business at the moment."

"Well, don't get your hopes up because I do have business to discuss." She sat in one of the wooden chairs facing his desk. She often wondered why he didn't have comfortable chairs in his office. "I think it's time for the men to make their own meals in the bunkhouse."

The returning rumble of laughter was not what she expected to hear.

"Why not?"

Her father laughed again. "Yep, you're here as my daughter."

She jumped up and folded her arms in front of her. "What is that supposed to mean?"

"It's simple. You don't want to be near Luke. Listen, honey, I know he broke your heart but you can't start changing the way we do things because you don't want to be around him. Frankly, I enjoy his company."

"Well, I'm certainly glad someone likes him. He's a washed up cowboy who is only good for sweeping the place." Hearing a gasp, she turned toward the door. Luke stared her right in the eye, straightened his back, then turned and walked away.

For the rest of the day she couldn't get the look on his face off her mind.

Meg pulled the roast out of the oven and placed it on the counter. "Ouch, oh damn!" She put her burned finger in her mouth.

"Need any help?"

She didn't turn, she knew his voice. "No, Luke, I don't need anything from you."

"I don't have much to give." The sadness in his voice touched her heart.

She slowly turned. His face matched his voice although for some reason she didn't think he knew. "Listen, I'm sorry about what I said earlier…"

"It's fine. I am washed up, but I'm trying to make my way back." He grimaced as he sat down on the ladder back chair. "I'll be out of your hair in no time."

"Ain't happening," her father said as he walked into the kitchen. "That smells great, Margaret Mary."

Her mouth hung open and for the life of her, she couldn't make it close.

"What ain't happening, Owen?" Luke asked.

"Luke, I want you to stay. That land I bought from your dad belongs to you. It's your birthright. Truthfully, I bought the land to hold on to it for you. I promised your ma I'd always look out for you."

Luke raised his eyebrows and a flash of fury crossed his face. The two men stared at each other until finally Luke nodded his head. "What about my mustangs?"

Meg stepped forward, her hands on her hips. "Oh no, don't even go there. It's bad enough I'll have to put up with you in my house. You are not touching my mustangs. If you're lucky you can view them from your land." She shot her father a look of disgust. How the hell had this all happened? Luke was supposed to get well and leave.

Something was going on between those two, and she was determined to find out what.

"I'm not very hungry. You two can serve up the meal can't you?"

Her father took a step toward her but she raised her hand warding him off. "Don't, I can't do this right now. I'll talk to you later, Dad."

She shot Luke one last glare and walked out of the house into the cool air. Those mustangs belonged to her now. She had paid for them with her own money. Just who did Luke think he was? And what the hell was her dad thinking?

They used that land for grazing. In fact, they'd expanded their herd of cattle because of that land. *Damn*, she worked so hard day after day building up the ranch and for what? So Luke could waltz in and take half plus her horses? Her hands clenched as she walked to her red pickup. She climbed in, gunned the engine and drove the dirt roads that led to her mustangs.

They were a sight to behold, these majestic, high spirited horses. She jumped out of her truck and opened the gate to the large pasture. Upon spotting her, many of the horses came toward her. They were so friendly, and she loved each one. They'd probably remember Luke, as loyal as they were. She sighed. At least the new additions didn't already know him.

How was she going to be able to live in the same house with the one man who'd broken her? She wouldn't avoid her responsibilities. The hell with him. Somehow she'd just ignore him. Maybe it was a good thing. She'd begun to feel sorry for him, and now she had the right to be angry with him again.

Luke clenched and unclenched his fists, as he watched Greg carry his belongings and place them into an empty bedroom in the main house. His helplessness drove him crazy. What type of man couldn't carry his own stuff? His strength improved a bit every day, but his patience was wearing thin. Being busy and useful was his usual way to be.

The only thing that sparked his spirit was Meg. The fact she didn't want him there made it worthwhile. His lips twitched remembering her temper.

It didn't really matter, he planned to gain control of his mustangs. In fact, he was looking forward to wrestling them from her. How he was going to do it, he hadn't a clue, but they would be his. It might even be fun to see the fury in her eyes again. It was strange but she'd hardened. She had a good command of the ranch but he'd expected a bit of his old Meg to still be there.

His Meg, who was he kidding? She'd never been and never would be his.

"All set, Luke." Greg shook Luke's hand.

"Thanks, Greg, I appreciate the help."

"You'll be up and around in no time. You're getting stronger every day. I think it's great Owen held on to your land for you. Busy making plans for it?"

"Dreams perhaps, plans are still a ways off."

"I hear you on that. Have a good one." Greg left closing the front door behind him. It was quiet in the house, but it was a calm easy quiet. A sense of peace washed over him, surprising him. There had been no peace for him since the day he'd left town.

The door opened and Meg walked in. She gave him a slight glare, took off her Stetson and threw it onto the wall peg. She never missed. She wore another dark T-shirt, and once again he wondered where her feminine side had gone to.

"All settled in?" She stared at him, her face expressionless. "Dad feels better with you here."

"And you?" He held his breath waiting for an answer.

Her guard went up and her face became hard. "Whatever Dad wants is fine with me. I figure we get you well, and you'll be good to go."

"Good to go. I've been wanting that myself for a long time. Thanks to you, I've started to regain my determination. I've been lost for a while."

She hustled into the kitchen and began pulling out pots and pans. "We do need to get one thing straight. Those horses are mine. They are on what I guess is your land now, but they belong to me."

"So you say. Did my father give them to you?"

Meg put her hands on her hips. "I'll have you know I had to give your father every penny I had and then some. I borrowed money from my dad, which I have paid back, so no your father didn't give them to me."

Luke grimaced. "I'm sorry. I should have known better. My father would never have given you or your family anything for free. I would like to see the mustangs when I'm up to it. I've missed them."

Meg tilted her head as though she was trying to puzzle him out. "I'll drive you over tomorrow to see them. The herd has grown and I think you'll be impressed with my progress."

"I'd like that." Perhaps they would find common ground with the horses. Anything so she didn't scowl at him constantly. How much had she paid for the herd? There was no way his dad would have given her a break on the price. His heart lightened, he finally had something to look forward to.

Chapter Two

The promise of seeing his horses encouraged Luke like nothing else. He showered and shaved without too much trouble then stared at himself in the mirror. His face was filling out and he didn't appear as weak. Despair still reflected in his eyes, and he didn't expect that to ever change. He halfheartedly chuckled. He'd said he wanted to see the mustangs when he was up to it, and Meg immediately told him she'd take him today. She was a kick even if she did give him disdaining looks.

A part of him longed to have her in his arms and a part of him felt guilty. What kind of man felt that way when his wife had been in her grave only a few months? He ached for his loss and damned his fate. The what-ifs were getting to him. What if they had left a few minutes earlier or a few minutes later? The accident would never have happened.

He'd loved his wife but not as much as she'd deserved. At least he'd been a good father to her girl. So many regrets, too many regrets, and they haunted his every thought. Long kept secrets revealed, changed the course of his life. He'd always thought Meg would be his future, but now it would never be. His heart and soul were too battered.

Walking toward the kitchen, he was surprised to hear himself whistling. His mustangs were waiting. Meg stood at the stove her back to him and God; her jeans fit her like a glove. She was just as he remembered, curvy in all the right places and sexy as hell. Looking never hurt, besides she didn't want him anyway, so it was just as well.

Meg turned and smiled. "Great, you're up."

He frowned and eyed her with suspicion. Why was she being so nice? "Anxious to see the mustangs."

"I bet a lot of them remember you." She put a plate of eggs, bacon, and toast on the table. "Sit and eat first."

Keeping his gaze on her, he sank onto one of the hard wooden chairs. What was she up to? The nicer she became, the more he wary he felt. He stared at her, trying to figure her out. Only a few days ago she wasn't speaking to him. Her blue eyes gave nothing away but there had to be a catch.

"Why exactly are you taking me to see the mustangs?"

"Because I'm nice."

Luke laughed. "Yeah, right. No, really?"

"If you must know, my dad is making me, and if it shortens your recovery time, it's an added bonus for me."

He pasted a smile on his face. "I knew there was a reason." He tried to sound cheerful but his heart lodged in his throat. What the heck was wrong with him? One minute he didn't have it in him to look at another woman and the next he pined for Meg.

"We should get going, Luke, I have a lot to do today."

He stood up and brought his plate over to the sink. "I'm ready."

Meg smiled as she drove Luke out to his land. Her glance kept straying to his handsome face, and she wondered why he appeared more appealing today. Maybe it was just the relief of getting him out of her house that attracted her.

His eyes widened, and he smiled when his land came into sight. "It's been a long time. I can't believe your father held this for me. I never thought to receive such a gift." He frowned and his shoulders slumped. "I don't deserve it."

Something wasn't right. Why was Luke so down on himself? Her concern for him grew and seemed to push all other thoughts out of her head. She shook her head, she wanted nothing to do with him. "The mustangs should be right around the next curve. There are twenty-one in all."

Luke whistled. "You've doubled the herd? That's amazing."

The horses came into sight, and Meg could feel Luke's excitement. The air was suddenly charged, and pride of her accomplishment swept through her. Luke grabbed her hand and held it on his lap. His big hands engulfed hers, and her desire for him scared her. Her emotions were on a rollercoaster, and she couldn't take anymore. She snatched her hand back and tightly held the steering wheel.

As soon as she parked, Luke was out of the truck and walking toward the horses. It didn't take much to catch up to him, and when she did, she steeled her heart against his tousled, brown hair blowing in the wind and his glowing blue eyes. There were plenty of sexy men in the world and she didn't need or want Luke. She'd already proven that she didn't need a man in her life.

Luke whistled loudly and half the herd came running to him. It was a glorious sight, all the beautiful big creatures crowding around him, saying hello. He greeted each one then stared at her. The sense of peace that emanated from him astounded her.

"I knew they'd remember you."

His boyish smile reached his eyes. "I was hoping. It's incredible considering I've been gone so long."

Swallowing hard against the pain, she nodded. "It has been a long time."

Luke opened his mouth, but she didn't want to hear whatever he planned to say. She could see the apology in his eyes, but she didn't want to hear any lame excuses for why he'd left.

"I'll introduce you to the rest of the mustangs." She patted a sturdy bay on his neck. "This is Achilles and this one here is Hestia." She gestured to the spirited dun mare.

Luke put his hand on her arm and turned her toward him. "You gave them Greek mythology names? I can't believe you continued what I started."

She shrugged. "It seemed natural."

Luke searched her eyes and nodded.

She held her breath. Hopefully there was nothing to see. She tried hard to hide her feelings at all times and had always felt confident that she succeeded. Until now. Luke had a way of getting under her skin.

"You've changed," he said, his voice soft and low.

"What's that supposed to mean?"

He hesitated. "You used to be easy to read. You wore your emotions on your sleeve. Now I don't know what you think except you want me gone. I can understand why. I mean I left you just as we were starting something good, something I had hoped would be permanent."

"Permanent?"

"You must have known how I felt about you. I was just waiting for you to grow up so I could start dating you."

Tears filled her eyes. All this time she had thought he didn't find her appealing. "You left without a word."

"I know, and I'll be forever sorry for hurting you."

Tears trailed down her face, and she closed her eyes willing them to stop. "Why?" Her voice squeaked.

Luke shook his head. "I wish I could tell you but I can't.

Meg wiped away her tears. "Can't or won't?" She waved her hand at him. "You know, don't, just don't. The whole town thinks I drove you away. I've lived the last five years with people whispering behind my back. I don't even bother going into town unless I have to. Now I'm foreman of this ranch, I'm perfectly content with my life. I do what I love, and people stay out of my way."

Luke's stare was intense. "Is that what you want? You want people to stay out of your way? Hell, Margaret Mary, I thought you'd gone on with your life. I expected to find you with a husband and babies. Even I got married." His face shuttered as he turned away.

Married? No one had told her. Her mouth opened but there were no words. She folded her arms in front of her trying to keep from flying apart and her stomach threatened to rebel. What a fool she'd been, thinking all this time that something tragic had happened to him, thinking he'd be back for her if he could, and the whole time he'd been married.

Of course, he would have dated while he'd been gone, but marriage... Her thoughts had never strayed that far. How stupid, of course he'd be married. If imagining it would have been too much for her, the reality was shattering. Her body began to shake, and she clasped her hands together trying to still herself. After a few large swallows it worked, but the lump in her throat stayed.

Well, where the hell was his wife now? She should be here wiping her husband's nose instead of leaving it to others. He had the gall to come here when he had a wife? Her stomach dropped. Was he planning to build a house on his land and live there, raising a family?

Everyone had told her to get on with her life but she refused to listen. *Damn my stubborn hide!*

"Where is Poseidon? I don't see him with the horses?" Luke's back was still turned to her and his voice sounded odd.

"Your father shot him after you left. That's why I bought the herd, not for you, but to save them."

Luke turned and studied her. She bit the inside of her mouth to keep from saying anything else. There was no way she was going to cry in front of him again.

"Well, best be getting back. I have a lot of work to do." She tried to summon a smile but failed, unnerved by Luke's stare. "Ready?" She turned and walked to the truck not waiting for an answer. The sound of footsteps assured her he was right behind her. It was going to be a long ride back. Damn, why did he have to live at the house? All she wanted to do was race in and confront her father. Surely, he knew all about Luke's marriage. What else had he been hiding from her?

"Slow down. You're driving like the devil is behind you."

She nodded but refused to look at him. "Perhaps he is."

Luke held on while Meg drove hell bent toward the ranch. *Damn it all to hell!* He'd hurt her again. She held herself rigid, and her face was full of fury, exactly the way she'd always reacted when she felt hurt.

Sighing, he looked out the passenger window at the rapidly blurring countryside. All he did was pile hurt upon hurt on her, and it wasn't what he ever intended. It wasn't time for explanations, and there was no way he would talk about his wife and daughter, not yet.

Closing his eyes, he still heard the sound of the car crash, windows shattering and metal screeching, bending against metal. He would never forget the horror on Mary's face right before impact and the way she stared lifelessly at him after. Jill's screams often echoed in his head; there was no hiding from them, but that was his penance for not keeping his family safe.

The authorities had ruled that the accident wasn't his fault but there must have been something he could have done to prevent it. Meg wouldn't understand about his marriage and why he stayed, or why he even got married in the first place. Mary was a good person, and she had deserved someone who could give his whole heart to her.

Ironic, the whole time he was with Mary, he had thought about Meg, and now he couldn't get Mary out of his mind.

He was going to lose Meg for sure, the odds had always been stacked against them. He glanced her way again; her face was set in stone, expressionless. Her knuckles were white from gripping the steering wheel so hard.

His throat felt dry and he coughed. "I wish there was something I could say to you, Meg. I'm sorry—"

"Save it, Luke. You are no longer my concern. I don't even know you anymore, and I don't want to know you."

A slap to the face would have felt better. His chest ached as his heart squeezed. Sorrow washed through him, not for himself but for everyone he'd let down. The burden of his decisions over the years threatened to crush him, but there would be no reprieve, no way out, no one to help him bear it. Meg parked the truck next to the barn and he touched her arm. She turned her head but looked everywhere except at him. "Thank you for saving the herd. I know you didn't do it for me, but thank you just the same. My father is not an easy man to go against."

Giving him a curt nod, she turned away and got out of the truck. The fact that she didn't slam the door surprised him. Owen was sure to get some flack, if the way she stalked into the house was any indication. Owen didn't know much more than he had a wife and daughter, who were both killed in a car accident. He'd never asked any questions.

Luke eased out of the truck and hesitated. Should he go into the house? He started walking toward it; he couldn't let Owen take the brunt of her anger. He hoped he could defuse Meg, but he knew it wasn't going to be easy.

Sure enough, he heard raised voices as soon as he stepped on the front porch. Luke wanted to turn and run, but it was his fault and he had to try to make it right. Straightening his shoulders, he walked into the house and headed right to Owen's office. How much would he have to reveal in order to soothe Meg? Maybe it was time for a fresh start, but he wasn't sure his heart could take it.

The look of relief on Owen's face as he walked in was all Luke needed. It was time to tell the truth as painful as it was. Well, most of the truth. He cleared his throat, and Meg spun on her heel, her mouth agape, her eyes narrowed.

Margaret Mary at her best. It gave him comfort that she hadn't changed all that much, at least not as much as she thought. Her hard exterior was all show.

"Listen, the reason you two are fighting is my fault. I know I owe you both the truth, but I'd like to talk to Meg about it first if you don't mind, Owen."

Owen gave him long stare and finally nodded. "I'll leave you two alone."

Meg glowered at them both and then nodded. She watched her father walk away. Folding her arms in front of her, she stared at him, waiting for him to speak.

"First of all, I want you to know that I never meant to hurt you."

Meg shrugged one shoulder.

"That night after our date, my father and I had a big fight. Words were said that could not be unsaid. Nasty, hateful words, and he told me to go. I was so hotheaded that I did just that, I left thinking I'd never look back, but I did look back, every day. I thought about you constantly wondering what you must have thought of me. At the time my pride got in the way, and I just couldn't come home."

He rubbed the back of his neck as the memory of his father's words clamored in his head.

"I moved to Colorado and did odd jobs, mostly ranch work. I was soon known as the best horse trainer around, and I was hired by the owner of one of the finest ranches in the county."

Meg's stance hadn't softened one iota.

"He had a daughter, Mary, who had tangled with the wrong man. He forced himself on her, hurt her and left. This was after he wooed her and told her he loved her. She was devastated and doubly so when she found herself pregnant. I have to tell you that Mary was a very sweet girl, but I never felt what I should for her when I married her."

"Why did you marry her?"

"I was sorry for her. She felt shamed and worthless. Her dad approached me with the idea, and I figured I'd never see you again. I married her, and we had a daughter named Jill. The whole time I was with Mary I thought of you. She deserved better than me. I tried to love her, and I did to a certain extent but, Meg, you were always in my heart. Six months ago, there was a horrible car accident and I lost them both. The police said the accident wasn't my fault but I can't shake the guilt I feel."

Her eyes misted as she walked across the room and wrapped her arms around him.

Meg laid her head on his well-muscled chest, listening as the beat of his heart increased. All these years she'd owned a piece of his heart and hadn't known it. He'd held a big piece of her heart as well. It felt so right, better than she'd remembered. He made her blood sing but he also made her feel too vulnerable. "I'm sorry for your loss," she said woodenly as she reluctantly pulled away from him.

Distance and time to think was in order; being so close to Luke, she couldn't trust her feelings. Part of her wanted to kiss him and tell him all was forgiven and perhaps they could start over, but she wasn't a young romantic girl anymore. The way her body tingled from his touch confused her. Bitterness and heartbreak had hardened her and she didn't know how to go back. Right now, she didn't want to go back. Her heart couldn't take it, and her pride wouldn't allow it.

"Thank you." The sorrow in his eyes was intense. He'd suffered; obviously, he'd suffered.

"I won't bring it up again. It's your business, and I don't have any reason to pry, at least not anymore." Her dad had been right in giving Luke a home. "I have a lot of work to do, so if you'll excuse me?" Meg turned and just barely stopped herself from running out of the house, a swift walk was the best she could rein herself to.

She always thought if she just had the answer as to why he'd left, the hurt would ease, but if anything the pain was sharper than before. Sure, he had good reasons, she supposed, but marrying another woman was too much for her brain to wrap around.

The barn was empty, and she made her way to Merry's stall. Meg opened the latch and let herself in, and Merry's neigh of greeting was the last straw. She put her arms around her horse and cried into her neck. She cried for the girl she'd been, the constant hurt she carried and her foolishness of waiting for a man who married another.

It was a sad ordeal Luke had faced, but now was her time to grieve for what could have been. There were still many unanswered questions, which she planned to let lay. She wished she could just move on, date perhaps, but the sting in her heart told her it wouldn't be anytime soon.

Merry's ears perked up, and Meg stood still, listening as Luke came into the barn. Like a coward, she ducked down until he walked by and then back out of the barn. Wishing him well was one thing, but seeing him every day was going to be a very long nightmare she wouldn't be able to escape.

Meg sighed as her tears finally stopped. The best way to avoid Luke would be to let him take charge of the mustangs. Her heart squeezed even more, creating excruciating pain, but it really was the only way. He did live in the house, but she would keep herself scarce. There was always plenty to do on the ranch. Hopefully, Luke would start building a house of his own soon.

Luke watched the mustangs with pride. It had been two weeks since Meg told him his job was to manage the mustangs. The hurt in her blue eyes haunted him, and he knew her reasoning; she wanted him out of her hair.

Dinnertime mainly consisted of just him and Owen eating some canned or frozen meal. Meg left the house early and came back after dark. She needed her space. He understood, but still it stung, he was the reason she couldn't enjoy her own home.

His strength was flowing back, and his injuries were healing. He still had a ways to go, but today he planned to ride one of his horses. It was time to sell off some of the herd, but he'd have to find a good time to mention it. He smiled. *Damn, she's a stubborn one.*

If that fateful fight with his father had never happened, he and Meg would probably be married with kids of their own. Closing his eyes, he took a deep breath, it was best not to go there. A visit to his dad at the nursing home hung over his head. It was expected by everyone that he go, but he really didn't want to see the son of a bitch who'd ruined his life.

Talk about tangled webs, both his and Meg's parents had woven one hell of a web of lies. He'd always felt so sorry for his mother, the way his dad treated her had been cruel, but her actions had started the chain of events. She'd always acted so virtuous, so pious, but knowing she'd had an affair with Owen made it hard to think of her in a good light.

Zeus came right over at the sound of Luke's whistle. A powerful animal, and he couldn't wait to ride him. "Come on boy, let's get you saddled. I need to feel the wind on my face."

Finally, Luke had Zeus saddled and ready to go. Getting up into the saddle was a bit challenging, his leg didn't want to cooperate, but he managed. Glorious, an appropriate word for what he felt on top of Zeus. No more doubts, he was going to be just fine.

Luke rode his land with pride; his dad had chosen well when he purchased it. He'd find a way to pay Owen back some day. Right now, he was land rich but cash poor. It would all work out. Selling some of the mustangs was the key, but dealing with Meg was going to be near impossible. Owen would know he was right but Meg, his spitfire Meg, was certain to balk.

Some of the fences between his land and the O'Brien's had been removed and it felt odd. He'd ridden these fences to make sure they were still up and in good condition most of his life but they had every right to make use of his land. The idea of swinging by his old house was tempting, but he didn't think he'd be able to get off Zeus and back on again. If the owners were around it wouldn't be polite to talk to them from atop of a horse.

Finally, he rode to the spot where his brother was buried. His heart panged for a life taken so young. David had been a rebel; if there was a way to piss their dad off, David had found it. Luke would like to believe that David and his mom were in heaven together, but he had his doubts.

Scanning the horizon, he spotted a rider and quickly left the gravesite. It was Meg. Even from this distance, he could tell. She had a gracefulness about her when she rode. Actually, it surprised him that she rode in his direction. These days all he saw of her was her back.

He spurred Zeus toward her, not wanting her to spot the place where David was buried. No one knew he was dead, and it was better for all involved to let it lay.

She rode toward him, and her smile surprised him. It probably wasn't for him. She was so beautiful with her long hair cascading freely down her back, and her tan Stetson was the perfect contrast for its sable color. Her carefree nature was missed.

"Howdy, Meg, what brings you out this way?"

"I thought I'd better take a look at my mustangs." She stared just left of him, avoiding his gaze.

"I see, going to take a head count?"

Her brow furrowed, and she cocked her head to one side. "Do I need to? Is there something you're not telling me?"

He wished he could tell her all of his secrets. "No, not at all, although we do have to trim the herd. You could get a lot of money for some of these horses."

To his surprise, she nodded. "I know. I guess in the back of my mind I've been waiting for you to come home. You have more knowledge about mustangs than I do. Let me know which ones and we'll discuss it." There was little emotion in her voice.

"You've done well with them. Most are saddle ready. Who did that for you?"

Her mouth hung open, and a glimmer of her feisty spirit showed in her eyes. "It was me and only me. I bought the mustangs on the condition that I would take care of them."

"You saddle broke them? I'm impressed, it's not an easy job. I've been thrown from more mustangs than I care to admit."

Nodding, she smiled slightly. "I've had my share of bruises and aches."

"You didn't come out here alone did you?"

"Of course I did. I'm the ranch foreman. I can do anything a cowboy can do, only better. I have to admit that the men weren't all thrilled but they've come around and respect me." She held her head up proudly.

The lusciousness of her lips hypnotized him.

"What is so interesting you have to stare?"

He gave her a wide smile. "You don't know how beautiful you are. I find you enchanting."

Cringing she shook her head. "Sweet talking me isn't going to work."

He winced.

"Are you okay? Is your leg hurting you?"

"Afraid I may be laid up and won't be able to work?" He couldn't help the sarcasm in his voice.

Her horse sidestepped and it took her a minute to get her under control. "To think I was actually concerned about you. I have work to do. Why don't you draw up a plan for the sale of the mustangs and we can talk in dad's office after dinner."

"I know you have work to do. In fact, you work too hard. After dinner sounds fine."

Meg nodded, turned Merry around, leaving him to choke on her dust as he watched after her.

Damn, why couldn't she just give an inch in his direction? It was going to take a whole lot of persuading but in the end, he planned for Meg to be his.

Later, Meg paced back and forth in her father's office. She'd skipped dinner, needing to think. Selling part of the herd was something she intended to do but there were never enough hours in a day to get everything done. In fact having Luke take over the mustangs had been a relief. She just hoped he didn't get hurt riding them.

A knock on the door stopped her pacing. "Come in."

The door opened slowly and Luke's expression reminded her of a boy waiting to see the principal. Was talking with her that painful? She gave him a slight smile. They used to be so easy together. Now it was almost too much effort.

She walked behind the desk and sat down. It felt odd, her father always sat here. "About the mustangs—"

Luke sat in the black leather chair near the fireplace, and that confused her. Was he taking this conversation too lightly? Was he dismissing her power as the foreman? Whatever his game, she wasn't pleased.

"I know that look, Meg, and before you blow a gasket, I'm sitting here because my leg hurts. Come sit next to me."

The fact that she hesitated saddened her. She was always expecting an ulterior motive to all his actions. Her stomach dropped a bit, but she stood up, grabbed her paperwork, and sat in the chair next to his. She had a right to her feelings, given his past behavior.

Luke cleared his throat. "I already had plans to sell half my herd before I left. I'd still like to do that. Then what I'd like to do is work with the mustangs you broke and trained to get a feel for their strengths and weaknesses."

"You doubt my training?"

Luke smiled and shook his head. "Of course not. I just haven't been able to ride until today, and I'm not going to sell a horse I haven't ridden. As far as I can tell, you did an amazing job with those horses." He winced as he shifted in his chair.

"You won't be able to ride them for a while. You probably shouldn't have been on Zeus today."

"I know, you're right, but I couldn't help myself. I just had to be on the back of a horse. You of all people should understand."

The smile she gave him was real, and it surprised her. "I know exactly how you feel. What if I took some time each day to ride the mustangs for you. You can tell how good they are by watching me."

Luke laughed. "Oh, Meg, I can't promise the horses are the only things I'll be watching. You sure are a nice distraction, but I think it will work."

"If I'm going to distract you—"

He gave her an intense stare, and she felt as though he could see her heart and soul.

"It was a compliment, Meg. This is the part where you're supposed to thank me. I'd think you'd be used to compliments, but I have the feeling you don't allow people to give them to you."

"Well, I'll let you know tomorrow what time I'll be able to ride." She stood up and hurried out of the office. She wasn't going to fall for his glib comments about her supposed beauty and what did he mean she didn't allow compliments?

Chapter Three

The next week went surprisingly smooth. Meg stopped by the mustang herd each day and rode for Luke. At first Luke stiffened when she rode up, and she had a feeling it was an ego thing. Other than the one time he'd climbed on Zeus, he hadn't been able to ride again and it made him impatient with himself and anyone else who happened to get in his crosshairs.

For some reason she enjoyed his grumpiness. He was fun to tease, and things weren't as awkward between them. Hell, she lived with the grouchiest of all men, worked with a few, too. His caustic nature was a buffer between them, and she was grateful. She didn't have to worry about compliments.

The Texas sun beat down as she rode Hestia. She was a beautiful mare with a dun appearance and black points. Pulling down the brim of her hat, she observed Luke. He still had a slight limp when he walked, and she knew he was trying to hide it from her. If she mentioned it, he hit the roof.

"What do you think?" she called out.

Luke nodded his head and actually smiled. "She's one of the best. We'll keep her and see what type of foals she throws. I have a feeling her offspring will be stars."

Walking Hestia toward Luke, Meg stopped and slid out of the saddle. "She's my favorite. When we decide which ones to sell, are we going to auction?"

"I have an idea some of my buddies I used to rodeo with might be interested. I'd like to give them first choice. If they get the word out, we might not have to go to auction. This way I can size up the buyer."

"No selling to jerks."

The corners of his mouth turned upward. "Exactly."

"I like your idea, Luke. I was wondering if you'd gone to see your dad yet."

Pain sparked in his eyes, followed by irritation. "I know I should, but I just can't look at that son of a bitch. To the whole town of Carlston he was a wonderful husband and father, but behind closed doors he was a cruel, abusive bastard."

Reaching out, she touched his shoulder. "I'm sorry you grew up that way. I've been blessed to have two devout parents."

Luke snorted.

"What?" She frowned. Something wasn't right.

"It's not my story to tell. There's a lot in life that isn't what it seems. People hide behind masks of their own making. Honesty and truth seem to be optional these days. I know I sound bitter, but that's how I feel."

He started to turn away, but she grabbed his arm. "Luke do you know something about my parents? I want to know."

He stared at her hand on his arm. "I'm not going to be the cause of hard feelings. It eats at your soul and once secrets are revealed, they can't be hidden again. Don't ask me, Meg."

Something akin to fear made her shiver. "I'll find out on my own."

He took her hand. "It's not important. I have to tell you that I was right. You have been a big distraction this week. You have a great seat in and out of the saddle."

His compliment wormed its way into her heart, and she blushed. "You just keep your eyes on the horses, not the rider. I'll see you later but this conversation is far from over. Inquiring minds and all."

"See ya later."

As she turned and walked to her truck, she could feel him watching her seat. She smiled her first real smile in days.

If there was a secret, she was determined to find it. Meg's belief in her parents wavered. What did Luke mean they had secrets? He made it sound ominous, and her gut clenched in unease. Drama, there was nothing she hated more.

When she got home, she found her father in his office. Taking a deep breath, she walked in. She crossed her arms in front of her and widened her stance, ready for anything.

"Hi, honey. I was just looking online at all the bulls for sale. It might be time for a new one." He glanced up and frowned. "What's wrong?"

Shifting her weight from one foot to the other, she wondered how to start. "I was talking to Luke."

"How's he doing with those mustangs?"

"Fine. I was talking to him, and he mentioned that you and Mom had some big secret. I got the impression that it was bad." From the ominous look on her father's face, she wished she hadn't asked.

"Sit down, honey. You deserve to know."

Meg eased into the chair in front of his desk.

"The fact is I had an affair with Luke's mom, Nancy. It was before you were born. We were both married and it was wrong."

Meg gasped.

"There's more. Nancy and I have a son, David."

"David is my brother? Did Mom know?"

He nodded his head slowly. "It was hard on both families. Your mom and I finally made peace with it. It was rocky for a long time, but we worked through it, and then you were born." He took a deep breath and let it out slowly. "Nancy and Harry's marriage was never the same."

"Did you love her?"

"She was my high school sweetheart. After we graduated, we went in different directions. I cared about her, and she was so unhappy in her marriage. But it was wrong."

"David doesn't know?"

"Well, since Luke seems to know I'm assuming David does too. That might be why he took off. I've had people look for him over the last few years, but there's been no sign of him. I wish we'd told him years ago, maybe he would have stuck around. I just don't know."

"This is so much to take in. I'm glad you and Mom worked it out. Luke's dad, Harry, used to hit them. I can see why Nancy was so unhappy, but you two toyed with Harry and Mom's life."

He suddenly appeared weary. "I know. I thought I was going to lose everything. It took your mom a long time to even talk to me, let alone forgive me. It's a part of my life that I'm ashamed of."

"No sign of David at all? Wow. I hope he turns up. But if he does, he's not taking my job as foreman."

"I promise."

Meg stood up and walked out the door. Suddenly her perfect upbringing was anything but perfect. Walking outside, she sat on the porch steps. Luke was right about a big secret. Damn him, why couldn't he have left things alone? Her foundation was shifting and it was his entire fault.

She jumped up from the porch step as soon as she spotted a truck driving up. There was no way she was talking to him. He should have told her the truth years ago. Everything she'd thought or felt before he left had been an illusion and it infuriated her.

Walking as fast as she could toward the west pasture, she heard his footsteps behind her. The twisting of her heart urged her to walk faster.

"Hold up, Meg, you know I can't walk that fast." His breathless plea got to her and she stopped.

Keeping her back to him, she stared out at the cattle. The ranch was her salvation. When all else went to hell, at least she had it to hang on to. His footsteps were near, and she finally turned around, determined to remain strong. The news was a blow, but she didn't want to show weakness.

His limp was much more pronounced, and he winced with each step. Damn, he was just the messenger. The only part he played was keeping the secret.

"Are you okay? Meg? I shouldn't have mentioned anything to you. I don't even know why I did. It serves no purpose, and I only got you hurt."

"I'm fine." She lifted her chin and gave him her best glare.

"You don't look fine, and you can stop giving me the look of the devil. Do you want to talk about it or would you like me to go to hell?"

"Go to hell?" Her shoulders slumped.

"Is that a question or a request?"

"Don't try to make me feel better. I had a good old fashioned wrath building up."

"Aw, honey, I'm sorry for everything. That was one of the reasons I left, you know."

Drawing her eyebrows together, she stared opened mouth at him and studied him. "You left because of my dad and your mom?"

"I'd known about that from the moment I was born. There was never an argument when David's parentage wasn't brought up. In fact, we were both warned to stay away from you. David disappeared, and it spurred me to finally take a chance and ask you out. That was part of what we argued about after I dropped you off and went home."

He walked closer to her and took her hand. "He threatened to ruin your reputation if I didn't stop seeing you. He backhanded me pretty good too. I knew I wouldn't be able to stay away from you if I was still in town, and I couldn't take the chance. My father is a mean old son of a bitch, and he'd eagerly smear your name around town. So, I took off and I'm sorry, but I thought it was for the best."

The plea for forgiveness in his eyes pinged her heart and she squeezed his hand. "It's all been a bit much to take in. I really thought my parents were, well I put them up on a pillar and they've been knocked off today. I don't know what the truth is anymore. Was my happy family a façade? I can't even think straight."

Luke pulled her into his strong arms and stroked her back. "I was selfish. I shouldn't have said a word, but it was killing me you didn't know why I left you. I loved you. I still do."

"I just wish I was a whole man instead of some yahoo trying to put his life and body back together. I wish I could forget about everything. Well truthfully, I can't say that. I did care for Mary in my own way, and I loved Jill as though she were my own. From the day she was born she had me wrapped around her little finger and ultimately became the light of my life."

Meg pulled out of his embrace and took his hand. "Let's get you sitting down. You need to rest your leg more."

Puzzled, he didn't say more, just held her hand the whole way home, wondering what was going on in that mind of hers. They made slow progress but finally they were in front of the house. The sight of the porch steps made him wince.

Meg let go of his hand and turned to face him. "I'm sorry about the way I've been acting. I've made everything about me, and I'm not usually a selfish person, at least I don't think I am. I've been so caught up in my own pain to even consider yours."

She climbed the few steps and then turned. "Come let's sit out here. I want you to tell me all about Jill. She sounds like a wonderful girl."

Somehow, some of the weight on his shoulders lifted. Glancing at her, he didn't find pity in her eyes. Instead he found compassion. Still he wasn't sure if he could really say much more about his baby without breaking down. He grabbed on to the railing, pulled himself up each step and finally eased himself down onto one of the cushioned wicker chairs.

Reaching out, Meg touched his knee. "It might help if you talked about it but it's up to you. Whatever makes you comfortable. We could just sit here without talking if you want.

"No one could ever accuse you of being selfish, Meg. I've only told you the bare bones of my life the last few years. I'm just hoping that time will ease the pain."

"Luke you know it doesn't work like that. Time does help but having the support of loved ones is invaluable. Have you tried to find David? I find it hard to believe he hasn't reached out to you. You two were so close."

He rubbed the back of his neck and glanced away. He'd found David, but he couldn't tell her. "Haven't heard a word from him." His pulse raced, lying didn't come naturally to him. Natural for his dad, but not for him.

"Well, I hope he turns up soon."

Trying not to cringe, he nodded his head. Finally, he turned toward her and gave her a ghost of a smile. "I'm glad I have you. I spent a lot of time in the hospital and doing physical therapy before I came here. Mary's dad came around but it was a very lonely dark time for me. The first few months I'd wake up yelling. The whole accident replayed in my mind but in slow motion, night after night. It was agony, pure hell."

"Oh, Luke."

"No feeling sorry for me or I won't be able to tell you more. I can't stand pity." Standing up, he reached out his hand. "Come on, I'm starving."

The next day Owen called Luke into his office. Owen smiled widely as Luke entered.

"Come in, I have a solution to all your problems." On Owen's desk was a map to Luke's property.

Curious, he stepped closer. "What might that be?"

"I got a phone call this morning from a land developer."

Luke started to object, but Owen put his hand up.

"Wait and hear me out before you say no."

Frowning, Luke nodded.

"This is a great plan, Luke. They only want the East corner of your property. I don't think that section has ever been used for much. You could sell, make a good penny, and then put all the money into cattle and a house. I see it as a win-win."

His heart beat so hard, Luke was certain Owen could hear it. "What do they plan to do with the property?" He held his breath.

"Build condos. What are a few condominiums? You probably won't even notice they're there."

"Condos? Owen, I appreciate all you do for me, but no one is digging up my land, and I certainly don't want people near my place." Luke sat down. If they started digging, they'd find David's body for sure.

"Listen, Luke, I know you have some money stashed away, but this could make life much easier for you. You could hire help and not ride."

Owen still sported a smile and Luke wondered if he even realized that he'd just stomped on his pride.

"Now if you're worried about your brother, we can hold back half the money for him to claim when he comes home."

Luke grabbed the arms of the chair until his knuckles turned white. Owen wasn't going to take a flat out no. He sighed. "I'll think about it, Owen, and I do appreciate you watching out for me. Parting with a piece of land is a hard thing to do, and it's going to take a lot of thinking."

Owen walked toward Luke and patted his shoulder. "Thinking is all I can ask." His voice sounded chipper as though it was a done deal.

Luke nodded until Owen left. *Holy hell, now what am I supposed to do?* Perspiration formed on his brow, and he took slow, deep breaths trying to calm his racing heart. If they found David's body, they'd blame it on him. He was an accomplice after the fact or something, wasn't he? He knew about the murder and kept quiet. Damn, he didn't even know how David had been killed. He'd always figured his dad had beaten him to death.

"Luke?" Meg stood in the doorway, pretty as a picture and he felt everything falling apart. He'd be in jail, and she'd eventually marry. The depth of his feelings astonished him.

Of course, he'd always loved her, and this time he wanted to fight to keep her.

"Dad told me what you two were discussing. You aren't going to sell, are you?" She sat in the chair next to him and took his hand, giving it a gentle squeeze before she let go.

"I told your dad I'd think about it."

"Luke, once sold you can't get it back. Dad says the land is good for nothing, but the mustangs run there. I know money is a concern, but I can help you build up your ranch. It might take more time than we think, but we can do it together." She turned red. "I mean if you want my help."

Leaning over he cupped her face in his hands and stared at her luminous eyes before he kissed her. Kissing her felt so right, and it eased his fears. He couldn't lose her. Her lips tasted of honey and reluctantly he pulled away before it deepened.

"I'll think about it for your dad's sake, but I really like the idea of you and me building it together."

Silence filled the room, and Meg was sure she'd said the wrong thing. Maybe she was pushing her way into his life. Giving him a weak smile, she started to edge around him, planning to leave.

"Hey, where are you going?" His sultry voice tugged at her heart.

"I…I have a way of bulldozing into other people's lives, and I can tell by your silence I've done it again."

Luke grabbed her hand. "I can't picture you bulldozing your way into anything. As foreman, I guess it could happen but not with me. I want your help, and I love the idea of you helping me. It's just you have so much to do already, and you put a full day's work here. I couldn't ask anything more from you."

If he hadn't melted her heart with his kiss, the words he spoke would have. Her hand looked so small in his large masculine one, and they were both work-worn. She'd been a naive girl when he'd left, now she was his equal.

"Cowboy, I have enough men working for me, and I don't have to work so hard. Before you came back, I split my days between ranch work and home. When you came back, I was still hurt you'd left, so I worked out on the ranch all day to tire myself out and keep my mind off of you."

"I'm sorry—"

She placed her finger over his delightful lips for a moment. "It's all good. You're back now, and that is all that counts." After giving his hand a quick squeeze, she let go and smiled. "I'll give you time to think about it. I actually do have a few things that I need to get done today. See you at dinner?"

"Yes, dinner sounds great."

His warm stare followed her as she left the room. Even if they didn't work together, she hoped he didn't sell any of his land. Her land ran through her blood, and she couldn't imagine selling an inch of it, but it wasn't her decision.

Walking outside she took a deep breath while staring at her land. She could bulldoze with the best of them. Hell, when Luke had left, she'd thrown such a fit about being the foreman she'd gotten Tony Blue fired. Now her actions shamed her. He was a good man, and he deserved the job he'd been doing for years.

Fortunately, she made her peace with Tony a year ago. Her dad made sure he got a good job with good pay but it had hurt his pride he'd lost his job. It wasn't easy going to his house, hat in hand, to apologize. At first he slammed the door in her face but finally he listened as she admitted how selfish and manipulative she'd been. He had accepted her apology, but they'd never be friends again.

Now she'd have to take a step back and allow Luke to make his own decisions. She promised herself she'd never meddle in anyone's life again. Hopefully, they'd end up with the same goal to build his ranch together.

A few days later, Meg glanced around the kitchen table, happy with the people in her life. Luke had gone out of his way to be a friend who was easy to be around. She even bounced a few ideas about improving the ranch off him. It was pleasant to be in his company except for the fact that she still waited for his answer. It would be a fine thing to build his ranch together, but it was his decision.

Owen placed two more pancakes on his plate. "Still my favorite, Meg. You would have made your ma proud." He gave her a loving smile then turned to Luke. I have assessors going over your east end this morning. I know you can't make an informed decision on that property until you know its value."

Luke turned pale. "What? They are on my property? Why didn't you tell me? I would have liked to have been there."

"If you hurry, I bet you can meet up with them," Owen replied.

"Dad, I'm going to head out with Luke. Can you handle things here?"

"Of course, been doing it for years."

Luke walked out the door so fast, she had to run to catch up with him. "Wait! I'm coming with you." She jumped into the truck.

The knuckles on his hands were white as he gripped the steering wheel. "Selling or not, I don't abide people on my property."

"I know and I agree, but my dad was just trying to help."

Gunning the engine, he nodded. "I know."

The beat of his heart echoed in his ears. He had to get to the east end first. If anyone started digging around, oh hell, he didn't know what they'd be doing but he hoped digging wasn't on the list.

Two pick-ups and a backhoe were parked on the edge of his property, and perspiration formed on his brow. At least there wasn't a police car there. Taking a deep breath, he tried to calm himself. He could pull this off; he didn't have a choice.

"Looks like we got here right in time. Might as well find out how much it's worth since they're here," Meg said as she opened the truck door.

What? When did she change sides? Shaking his head, he got out of the truck.

A tall man in a business suit walked right to them with his hand out. "I'm—"

Luke shook his hand. "Hey Ray, long time no see. So you appraise property?"

"Good to see you, Luke, Meg. I'm the land developer."

Luke's stomach clenched. "Why is there a backhoe here?"

"I'm sure you can understand I need to know what I'm dealing with. I need to know if the land is rock, and if so how far down it goes. It's all about costs."

"I'm not selling, Ray. I'm afraid you made a trip out here for nothing."

Ray frowned and turned to Meg. "I thought your father held title to this land."

She quickly glanced at Luke then smiled at Ray. "Well, yes he does hold the title but he kept it for Luke to have when he came back, David too."

"Sorry Luke, I need to call Owen and see what he wants me to do."

"Seriously? My word isn't good enough?" He sounded like a wounded bear, but he didn't care, he needed them off the property.

"Luke, you know it isn't like that. Listen, why don't you and Owen hash it out then give me a call. I have no desire to upset you. It's good to see you again." Ray shook his hand and tipped his hat at Meg. He started to turn but turned back. "Where is David? Did you ever hear from him?"

"Not in a long time." His world was beginning to close in on him.

Ray smiled sympathetically. "Well, hopefully soon then. Call me with your decision."

"I will, thanks." There wasn't any other choice; he'd have to move the body. The thought of disturbing David's resting place made his stomach lurch. He'd spent his whole life covering for his father, and here he was doing it again. People had seen the bruises on the Kelly boys and their mom. He'd learned at a young age to keep his mouth shut. Once when he told a teacher, his father took a hammer and broke his thighbone. That incident was the falling off the roof excuse and it kept him out of school for a while. When he returned to school, his teacher gave him looks of pity. He'd hated that.

Gym class was the worst, trying to change without anyone seeing his whip marks and bruises. Poor David had had it worse, and he had just refused to participate in gym class. The gym teacher called their house, and they came to a compromise. David would run laps after school every day. Closing his eyes, Luke could still remember David's back looking like raw meat by the time their father was done with him.

"Luke?"

"What?"

"I was asking if we should go." Meg took his hand and gave it a squeeze. "What are you thinking about? The pain on your face was intense."

"Just missing David is all. I wish he was here."

"Me too. I would have liked to have known my brother better."

"He was a good protective brother. It's a damn shame he's gone." Luke scanned the land until he came across David's grave. He was a good brother who had paid the ultimate price.

He smiled at Meg. "Let's go. I need to talk to Owen." He drove until they were about halfway back and pulled off the road.

"Luke, is something wrong?" The worry on her face warmed his heart.

He reached out and stroked her cheek with the back of his hand. "If I had the choice I'd have you by my side building the ranch, but I don't know what the future holds. I do know that I need to kiss you." Staring into her eyes, he leaned over and put his lips on hers. She immediately sighed and kissed him back, opening her mouth for him. She tasted like coffee and maple syrup. Deepening the kiss, he drew her closer to him, running his hands up and down her spine as she stroked the back of his neck and ran her fingers through his hair.

"Mmmm, you're a great kisser," she whispered against his mouth. "I don't understand it, but I want to get naked with you."

Breaking the kiss, he held her close to him, burying his face in her hair. She smelled of lavender. Was that her shampoo or her perfume? He waited for his heart to slow before he pulled away. "Naked would be wonderful, but not in the truck."

"You know if we keep waiting for the perfect place it'll never happen."

He gave her one of his cocky grins. "Don't you worry, darlin' when there's a will there's a way. I'm more than willing."

It wasn't as though she hadn't been attracted to other men, but she wanted Luke with a ferocity she couldn't understand, and his *taking their time* thing was making her crazy. A little loving in the truck would have been just fine for her, but Luke wanted to wait.

Most men would have had her flat on her back in no time. She got out of the truck at the same time Luke did. She didn't want him to touch her by helping her down . Her nerves were on high alert as it was.

"Going in to talk to Dad?" she asked.

"Yes, are you coming?"

"No, Luke, I have some things that need tending. See ya." It took a lot to restraint to keep from running into the barn. She paced her steps evenly, and once in the barn she sighed in relief.

Maybe he wasn't as into her as she was into him. What about the smoldering glances he sometimes sent her way? Damn, she wished she had more experience with men. She could always ask the hands, Ron and Greg their thoughts.

Biting back a chuckle, she shook her head. What was she thinking?

Sure, they enjoyed each other's company, but Luke had lived a completely different life while he was away. Too many things were coming at her all at once, and her predictable life was changing. Sleeping with Luke might be jumping the gun. Damn, she wanted that man.

Imagining him as a dad gave her pause but at the same time, she could picture it. Her emotions were awhirl. Happy he experienced having a child, horrified that his wife and daughter were dead, and jealous that he loved another woman and her child.

She led Merry out of her stall. "You know girl, my mother always said not to cry over spilled milk. Dad always said there was no closing the barn door after the horse had already bolted."

Meg saddled Merry and they were off. She rode out to see how Ron and Greg were doing with the downed fence. Seeing they were about done, she rode in the direction of Luke's property. She hadn't checked on the mustangs in days.

"Hold up, Merry." She sat on the horse marveling at the sight of the beautiful horses. She felt the same awe every time she saw them. They were so strong and spirited. Riding past them, she rode to the east end of the property and was stunned.

The backhoe on the property was surrounded by the sheriff and the state police. There were four cars with their lights flashing. What in the world was going on? Carefully, she rode toward them and as soon as she was close, an officer held her reins while she slid off the saddle.

"What's going on?" she asked the officer.

The officer looked over her head toward the sheriff. Turning she saw him nod.

"We found, well not we, there's a body buried on the property."

"There's probably bodies buried all over Texas. It is a state with a colorful history."

The officer shook his head. "This one isn't all that old. Hard to tell but the baseball bat buried with the body is a light grade aluminum bat. They started making those is the '90s—the 1990s."

Meg shook her head trying to clear it. "What? I've ridden over this parcel a million times and I never saw a grave. Wow, a grave?" Her heart skipped a beat as she wrapped her mind around the news.

The officer blocked her attempt to move around him. "You can't go any closer. It's a crime scene," he told her giving her a speculative look.

"A crime scene," she repeated. "Don't look at me that way, and you'd better not try to add me to your persons of interest list either. No one from around these parts would bury a body here." Grabbing the phone out of her pocket, she turned away from the officer.

"Who are you calling?"

"My father, I believe he is the legal owner of this property."

The officer's brown eyes narrowed.

"It wasn't my father either. Good Lord, what cop shows have you been watching?"

She glared at him until he had enough sense to turn away. After speaking with her father, she walked back to the officer and Merry. "Do you know who it is? What happened? Do you have any leads?" She grabbed Merry's reins from the tall, lean officer with short blond hair. "What did you say your name was?"

"I'm Detective Timbers."

"Detective? No, I don't think so. You're too young, and if you really are a detective you'd be down there examining the scene." She flashed him a cocky smile.

"Listen, Meg, I have—"

"How do you know my name?" She dropped Merry's reins confident the horse would stay, placed her hands on her hips and scowled.

He smiled widely. "I'm a detective, remember?"

"Oh, for Pete's sake! Okay, you're a detective but seriously how do you know my name?"

"You were described by the sheriff as pretty, feisty, and bossy, and I have to say it's a very accurate description of you."

"If you say so," she replied, her voice laced with sarcasm. "Do they know who it is?"

He shook his head. "Can't comment on that."

"Could you at least get Sheriff Newman? I'd like to speak to him."

Detective Timbers whistled through his teeth at the crowd of law enforcement huddled around the body. Sheriff Newman looked up, nodded and walked toward them.

"Just like that, you whistle and he comes?"

He winked at her. "Newman and I are cousins."

Great, just great. She took a deep breath and let it out slowly as she watched the sheriff make a path to them. She'd known him all her life and when she was just a girl, she had asked him to marry her. Tall, dark, and handsome with a smile that could set a woman's heart pumping. Too bad he was twenty years her senior.

His fingers touched the rim of his hat as he nodded. "Good to see you, Meg. Wish it was under different circumstances."

"Nice to see you too, Wayne. Should I call you Sheriff Newman?"

He gave her one of his famous smiles and shook his head. "Wayne is fine. After all we were almost engaged."

Feeling the detective's stare, she suddenly found her boots to be very interesting while her face heated. *Hell*, why did Wayne always tease her? She shuffled her feet a bit then glanced up. "Too bad it didn't work out. We'd probably have a passel of kids by now."

Wayne laughed. "Very true, darlin'."

Detective Timbers shook his head. "Well, I guess I don't know everything about you after all," he admitted.

"What's going on, Wayne? Timbers here said there's a body buried on this land."

"Detective Timbers, not Timbers."

Meg ignored him and kept her gaze on Wayne.

"Ward probably told you everything we know."

"Ward?"

"Detective Timbers, not Ward and not Timbers."

"Fine, whatever. Here comes my dad and Luke."

The closer Owen drove to the site, the more gut sick Luke felt. Perspiration dotted his brow, and he desperately tried to slow his breathing, hoping it would slow the racing of his heart. This was it, the moment he prayed would never come. He blinked a few times when the police cars with their lights glaring came into view.

"Wow, looks like they got the whole posse here," Owen exclaimed.

"It sure does. What did Meg say exactly when she called?"

"Just what I told you, there's a body buried up here. If she knew more, she would have told me. Look there's Wayne, he'll know what's going on." Owen parked the truck, and they both got out. They didn't have to take many steps before Wayne and another officer approached them with Meg following closely behind.

Meg ran past the two men into her dad's arms. Luke wished she'd run to him, but it was just as well she drew comfort from Owen; They'd need each other.

Strong and steady. These next few minutes could determine his life, and jail wasn't an option he was willing to entertain.

"Hey, Wayne." Owen reached out and shook the sheriff's hand. "You remember Luke Kelly, don't you?"

Sheriff Newman nodded and shook Luke's hand. "Good to see you back." He sighed as he sized them up. "We have a problem, and I'd like to get this solved as quickly as possible."

Spotting the backhoe on the property, Luke's heart sank. He shoved his hands in his pockets. How was an innocent person supposed to act? "What happened?"

"Found a body buried, Luke. All we know is a female is lying in a grave, and a bat was buried with her. I don't see many homicides, so I called in the state police. This is Detective Timbers. He will be heading up the investigation."

Luke nodded to Detective Timbers and swallowed a lump that formed in his throat. A woman? Who the hell was buried out there? Timber's eyes narrowed as he stared at Luke. Damn, he was in the detective's cross hairs.

"A female?" Owen asked, perplexed.

"Yes. I can't think of anyone who'd gone missing, but the state police have better access to national information. Hopefully we can ID her easily enough."

If not David, who was buried? At least he didn't have to pretend to be in shock it was real. Where the hell was David buried? It had been dark when he and his dad...

"Luke, are you okay?" Meg touched his arm.

Looking down into her compassionate eyes, he felt like a fraud. This would be the perfect time to come clean about David, but selfishly he wanted Meg to always look at him without hate.

Placing his hand over hers, he gave her a small smile and a nod. "It's so unbelievable. Who found the—the body?"

"Ray had his crew out here to assess the land. He tells me Owen sold it to him," Wayne said.

Owen frowned. "I haven't sold anything yet. In fact, I was holding the land for Luke and David, but Ray called and said he had the backhoe and crew already here and I gave him the go ahead." He turned to Luke. "I know you told Ray, no but I thought you should know your options."

Detective Timbers smiled. "Good thing or we'd have never found the body." He still eyed Luke.

Meg squeezed Luke's arm. "Good thing, Dad. Maybe we can get her back to her family."

"I suppose I don't have to give the don't-leave-town speech to you." Detective Timbers smiled but his voice was serious. "I'll swing by in about an hour. I need a few questions answered."

Kathleen Ball

Chapter Four

The next day Luke got a call from Owen asking him to come to the main house. He and Greg had been herding the mustangs away from the burial site. Greg was good people. He did his job, did it well, and didn't ask a lot of questions. They put the two quarter horses they'd been riding into the horse trailer, and Greg drove them toward the main house.

Luke stared out the window feeling gut sick. He'd had the same feeling since he found out about the burial site and when they'd told him it was a woman he felt gut kicked on top of being gut sick, and it was a nasty combination. All night he lay in bed, tossing and turning, wondering who the woman was.

He tried to relax against the back of the truck seat, but his muscles were too corded to relax. "Hope it's not Detective Timbers again."

Greg looked at him briefly and nodded. "It's a tough one all right. That there Timbers guy wasn't so bad, though he did seem to have his eyes fixed on you. You probably weren't even here when it happened, but he has a job to do like the rest of us."

"I suppose he does, but I didn't like the way he eyed me either."

Greg turned into the long driveway to the house. "I don't see his car."

As soon as Greg parked, Luke got out of the truck, wincing. Riding still hurt his leg and hip. Spotting Owen on the porch, he silently swore. It must be bad if Owen was waiting for him out front.

"Glad you made it back so quickly, Luke."

"It sounded important."

"I got a call from the nursing home. Harry wants to talk to you."

Luke shook his head in confusion. "My dad wants to see me now? I got the impression he had no use for me. He never tried to contact me."

Owen shrugged his broad shoulders. "From what I gathered, he doesn't have his own phone." He tossed his keys to Luke. "Take my truck and tell him hello from me."

Luke caught the keys and nodded. He would have liked to clean up a bit but somehow he wasn't given an option. His dad must have heard about the body. Maybe he'd find out where David was buried, exactly. What a big mess and all he could do was sit back and watch.

He'd been plenty tempted to go back there last night to see if he could find David's body but he'd watched enough cop shows to know that they probably had someone staking the place out. He rubbed the back of his neck as he drove. He didn't want to see his dad and wished he could just forget everything that happened. *Damn*, if his father had killed David so easily maybe he'd killed the woman, too.

What about Meg? They wouldn't have a future when the truth got out. Taking a deep breath, he tried to calm himself before he got to the home. He didn't want to come off as suspicious to the staff. He parked the car, got out and then hesitated. This was bound to be a whole can of worms.

"You know your pacing isn't going to make Luke come home any faster," Meg's father said with a hint of worry in his voice.

There was no way she could stand still while waiting to hear what Luke's dad had to say. "Do you think Harry has any information about the body?"

"I'm sure Detective Timbers already questioned him. I think we would have heard if he knew something. You have to remember part of that land is heavily wooded and probably wasn't used for much. Anyone could have buried a body there."

The sound of an engine caught her attention, and she made a beeline for the front door. "He's here." She didn't wait for a reply before she flew out the door.

Luke's face stopped her short, and she stared. It looked as though he'd aged in the few hours he'd been with his father. She'd swear there were deep worry lines on his face. His eyes had dulled and his lips pressed together in a grim expression. "Luke?"

Slowly he shook his head. "The old bastard didn't have much to say. He seems to be off his rocker. His memory is spotty. " Shrugging his shoulder, he kicked up some dirt avoiding her gaze.

Heartsick, she let it go and didn't ask him anything else. He was keeping something from her, something big, and it didn't sit well with her. Ever since he'd come back he'd been slow to tell her about his life, which was understandable, but keeping things from her now…

"If you need anything or someone to talk to I'm here."

His gaze met hers and he shook his head. "There's nothing to tell." He walked by her and went into the barn.

The urge to follow him swept over her, but she stood in place. Could be his father was just an old bastard and they argued about the past. Maybe Harry was harboring a grudge because Luke had left. With both his sons gone, he'd hired more men to work the ranch.

Sighing, she went back into the house. Her dad was waiting at the window.

"It didn't seem as though Luke had much to say."

"He didn't. I think he's keeping something from me."

"Honey, he's a grown man with his own life, and he doesn't have to report to you," Owen said gently.

His words hit her hard. "I'll be upstairs if you need me." Hurrying to her room, she closed the door and leaned against it.

Her dad was right, and here she was making a fool of herself wanting to be intimate with Luke. She'd gone against everything she had learned about men and allowed him into her heart. How could she have been so stupid and so blind? He'd just lost his wife and daughter and foolishly, she'd told him she wanted him.

Something happened with his father today, and she was worried but it was time to admit that it wasn't any of her business. They'd sell half the mustangs and Luke could build his own ranch, she already had her place in life, one she'd been comfortable in before he'd come back.

A lone tear trailed down her face and she quickly swiped it away. She was the ranch foreman and foreman didn't cry. For now on her main concern was the ranch and only the ranch.

Up before dawn, Luke dressed and left the house. It was no use trying to sleep. Once again his whole world had been turned upside down, and he had no idea how to make it right again. Was a little peace in his life too much to ask? Things were going well with Meg, he'd finally gotten under her skin, and he looked forward to the unfolding of their relationship.

His leg hurt making his limp worse than ever. How was he supposed to act as though he knew nothing? Damn his father. Scratching his whiskered jaw, he wondered what was next. The best thing for everyone concerned would be if he could just disappear.

The worst of it was he'd been blind to it all, utterly clueless. A huge part of him couldn't believe it true. David couldn't have killed that woman and more, according to his father. Not the big brother he knew. David tried his best to keep him safe from their father's wrath. David had taken more than one beating for him.

He limped to the tack room and took a seat. Sighing, he ran his hand over his face. How many bodies were buried on the property, and were they all at the east end? The magnitude of his father's confession resonated through him until he felt sick. The brother he knew healed animals and couldn't tolerate any type of mistreatment of them. How could he be a serial killer? Now more than ever he wished he'd gone to the police the night of David's death.

Rubbing the muscles in his leg gave him a small measure of relief but he wouldn't be able to sit a horse. The way he brushed off Meg's questions the night before had hurt her, but it was unavoidable. She didn't deserve to be mixed up in his mess, and he wished he never tried to get her back. He should have left her alone, bitter but not tainted by his family. And poor Owen looking for David all these years, none of it was fair, none of it was right.

There hadn't been one sign of David's duplicity and surely, there would have been something. Why hadn't his father gone to the police instead of allowing it to happen repeatedly, knowing that there were at least ten bodies buried?

The creaking of the barn door brought him out of his musing, and he sat up straighter, trying to put a normal expression on his face. *Hell, what was normal, anyway?*

"Luke?" The worry in her sweet eyes almost brought him to his knees. "I brought you some coffee. I heard you pacing most of the night..."

He took the offered coffee and tried to conjure up a smile, but he failed. "I'm sorry. I wasn't aware you heard me. Did you get any sleep?"

Meg shook her head. "Not much, but I'm fine. What about you? Truthfully you don't look so good."

"I'm not feeling so hot either."

Meg took a step toward him and touched the back of his hand. Luke stared at her hand, feeling the warmth it contained. His heart saddened, all hope for a future with

Meg was gone. He'd known it but it hit extra hard with her standing in front of him looking so concerned.

He slipped his hand out from under hers and gave her a sad smile.

"If there is anything you need, all you have to do is ask. You know that, don't you?"

Why did she have to be so beautiful? "I know. I just need to work a few things out in my mind."

"I know you went to see your father and it must have been hard to be in the same room with a man who beat you. It might help if you talked about it. I'm here and I'm a good listener." Her concern made him hurt more.

"I can't talk about it, and I certainly don't want to taint you with stories of my father. He didn't know anything about the body." He quickly averted his gaze afraid his eyes would give away his lies.

"I didn't imagine he knew anything. He may be a mean son of a bitch but he's no killer."

Luke choked on his coffee. He coughed a few times and stared at her. "He is a mean son of a bitch."

"You were visiting him for a long time, certainly you talked about a lot of things."

His lips formed a grim line. "Let it be, Meg."

"I want to help you. I think talking about it will help."

The pounding of his heart echoed in his ears, there was no way he could let her know anything. "I already told you once, I don't want to talk about it."

"But—"

"Margaret Mary, what does it take for you to take a hint? I don't want to talk to you. You are one stubborn busybody, and I don't want to be around you. You push and push, and I don't find it attractive. In fact I find it downright ugly." His voice was louder, meaner than he intended but he had to get it through her head.

A flash of pain lit her blue eyes and then they dulled as her shoulders sank. She took a deep shaky breath, and nodded. "If that's the way you want it."

"I do." He stood, crossed his arms in front of his chest and watched as she flew out the barn. It was better this way. Wasn't it?

Part of his heart flew out the door with her but it was unavoidable. He'd been barely holding on, trying to regain himself each day and now this. How much was a man supposed to take before he couldn't take anymore?

At the sound of police sirens, he made his way slowly to the barn door. He sighed when he spotted Timbers walking his way.

"We found another body, another female. I think we'd better have a long talk."

Luke nodded and got into the car with Timbers hoping he'd be back home sooner than later.

Meg couldn't get the devastation on her father's face off her mind. They'd heard the sirens and watched Luke get into the police car while Timbers walked in their direction to tell them about another body buried in the same area as the first.

Giving her dad a quick hug, she saddled Merry and rode out. Luke was on his own this time. No one had ever called her a busybody before, and for damn sure she wasn't one. The heck with Luke Kelly and his thick, stubborn, stupid hide. Just who did he think he was? She'd let him have too big a voice about the ranch, but from now on it was her ranch, her rules. If he didn't like it, he could go pitch a tent on his own property.

She slowed Merry to a walk and wiped the perspiration on her brow with a bandana. She had to admit his words stung. Foolishly, she let him get to her, again. Her friendship with him wasn't working at all. If he stayed on, he'd have to learn she was the boss.

Scanning the horizon, she smiled at all the grazing cattle in her view and satisfaction rolled over her. This was all due to her and all the hard work and long hours she put in. No distractions were needed.

She patted Merry's neck after she swung out of the saddle. Maybe she should have stayed home with her father. The implication of a serial killer was bad enough but when you added David's disappearance, unwanted scenarios swirled through their heads. She couldn't picture David hurting a woman. He'd always been the type who took in strays.

What did she know? Hell, she'd just found out David was her brother. She led Merry toward a big white ash tree and sat under it, her back against the trunk. Her heart squeezed. Luke's comments hurt more than she thought and it didn't matter how many times she told herself they couldn't be together a small kernel of hope had existed in her heart that perhaps they did have a future together.

"I love him." Merry gazed at her, and then promptly turned away. "I know, I'm already suffering the hurt from my traitorous heart but I can't seem to let go. I think the problem is I don't know how."

Her eyes watered and she tilted her head back, refusing to cry. Finally, she stood up, wiped the dirt off her back and swung back up into the saddle. She'd been selfish to leave her dad alone. He needed her. Damn, where was David? And why hadn't they been aware two women had been missing?

She'd concentrate on her dad and the ranch, and stay out of Luke's business even though it meant giving up working with the mustangs just as long as she eventually got her investment back. Her heart didn't feel lighter after her decision.

As she rode toward the house, she groaned spotting Luke on the porch. He quickly came toward her and she groaned again. She didn't want to hear anything he had to say. Ignoring him, she slid off Merry and proceeded to take her into the barn.

Ron stepped forward and solemnly took Merry's reins. Something was wrong, and when she finally turned and looked at Luke, his eyes were full of grief.

He took her hand and held her in place not allowing her to go to the house. "No!" she wailed as she shook her head. But she felt it, like a stone around her heart. Her dad was gone.

"I'm so sorry, Meg." Luke gently took her into his arms and held her close.

She allowed it only for a second, maybe it wasn't true. She broke free and ran into the house. The first thing she saw was blue latex gloves on the floor near her father's favorite chair. Furniture had been moved, probably to make it easier for the medics to work on him.

"What hospital?"

"Sweetheart, he didn't make it."

"He was fine when I left him. Luke, he can't be dead. I need to see him." Her heart squeezed painfully.

"Hopefully we can see him tonight."

Her mind blanked. "Tonight?"

"We can go to the mortuary. I'll be heading there in a bit to bring clothes."

Meg sank into the nearest chair while staring at Luke and trying to make sense of his words. Tears streamed unchecked down her face, and every time she tried to stop, they flowed heavier. Running her hands over the smooth coolness of the leather chair's arm, she was finally able to take a deep breath.

"Can I get you anything?" He knelt in front of her, and his eyes held so much pity it made her cry all the harder.

Her whole world crumbled. What would she do without her dad? "If I had been here…"

Luke encased her hands in his. "It was most likely a stroke. The paramedics said it was fast and quick."

"They always say that."

He stood, grabbed a box of tissues and handed it to her. "I'm going to get his suit and stuff."

"No!"

"I'm sorry, of course you want to do it yourself."

Meg took a deep breath and little by little, she regained her composure, from here on, she needed to put on a brave face. "No, Dad wanted to be cremated and his ashes spread over the land. I know it sounds strange but—"

"No, it doesn't sound a bit strange to me, in fact, I understand completely. I'll call Howard and tell him about the cremation."

She sighed and nodded. "Thanks." She wished she was numb, but incredible pain spread throughout her body. Time for sorrow would have to come later because she had a ranch to run.

She stood straight and tall and glanced at Luke wondering how she was going to keep him at arm's length now. "Have all the men been notified?"

"Yes. They were here when the ambulance came."

"Well, then the next order of business is to get all of my dad's papers in order. I'll need to change the deed to the ranch to my name. I'm sure there are a million things I need to do."

Luke gave her a sad smile and was in front of her in two steps. He hauled her into his arms and held her tight. "That can all wait. You need to take time for yourself." He stroked her back with his powerful arms. Except for his limp, he seemed to be getting stronger and back to the Luke who left five years ago.

She allowed herself a small measure of comfort before she pulled away from him. "It needs to get done. I'm on his bank accounts so people will get paid and hopefully it will be business as usual."

Meg wrapped her arms around her middle and walked to the front window. A feeling of loneliness swept through her, but she suspected it was normal. It would be so easy to lean on Luke, but it would only lead to heartache. She was strong and that's the way her father raised her. It wouldn't be too big of a leap from foreman to owner.

Luke ran his fingers through his hair. Every time he tried to help Meg, she turned away. It had been a week since they'd scattered Owen's ashes, and Luke had tried to be there for Meg at every turn without success. He sat at the kitchen table, a glass of whiskey in front of him, waiting for her to come home. It was well after dark, and he was beginning to worry.

She must have turned her cellphone off because all he got when he called was her voice mail. The old house was too quiet. The clicking of the second hand on the green kitchen clock was the only sound. Frankly, he'd been waiting for her to ask him to move out but so far, she hadn't said a word about anything.

The light in the barn turned on indicating Meg was home. Everything inside him longed to go out there to help her, but he knew she'd only rebuff him. He sipped his whiskey and waited until she finally came through the door.

The large circles under her eyes were proof of many sleepless nights. She gave him a tight smile as she hung her hat on the wooden peg by the door. "I'll have a whiskey if you're offering."

"Sure thing, take a seat and rest." If only he had the right to pull her into his arms and comfort her, but he didn't.

He poured the whiskey and handed it to her. "Rough day? You don't usually drink whiskey."

Meg swallowed hard then drank the whiskey down fast. "You could say that. I have missing cattle, cut fence lines, the police are too busy looking for whoever killed those women. I named Greg Sparks the new foreman, and

I had three of the men quit. I guess they all expected they were meant to be the foreman."

"How many cattle?"

Sighing she shook her head. "I can't get a count. They've all been scattered but near as I can tell, at least two hundred. It could be more, I just don't know. Plus I don't have the manpower to replace the fencing and count heads."

"Meg, why didn't you call me? I would have come."

Still shaking her head, her eyes filled with tears, which trailed down her face. "I don't know."

Luke stood and pulled her up. He stared into her eyes waiting to see any sign of rejection and when he didn't see it, he pulled her to him and held her close. He stroked her hair as she cried into his neck. Her body shook with her sobs.

"I'm here." He kept her in the enclosure of his arms for a long time, until she finally stopped crying.

Slowly, she pulled away just enough so she could see his face. "Thank you, Luke. I don't know what came over me but, well, thank you."

"I'm always here for you when you need me."

"I know. I just wanted to stand on my own, and I was doing a good job until today."

"Oh, honey, today wasn't your fault. You do need to figure out a plan to have the fences watched."

"We need to figure it out."

"We?"

She nodded. "I'm asking for your help. I can't do this alone."

"You know I'll help you." He pulled her back against him and held her.

Her body was well toned, yet so soft, sweet, and supple in his arms. Her hair smelled like sunshine and everything green from the grass to the trees. Luke closed his eyes cherishing the feel of her against him.

His whole body hummed, but he decided to take it slow. He wasn't going to lose her trust this time or make her run in the other direction. He'd loved his wife, Mary, but it hadn't been the profound love he held in his heart for Meg.

She wrapped her arms around his waist and laid her cheek against his chest while he rubbed her back. Finally, she tilted up her face as though expecting a kiss but Luke just smiled and kissed her on the cheek.

The questions in her eyes almost had him, but he needed to stay on course. He loosened his hold and took a step back. "You know I'd do anything for you. Who do you have guarding the downed fence area?"

"Greg is out there now, and Ron will spell him at dawn. Greg rode out and sent me home, that's why I'm so late." She sat at the kitchen table and sighed. "I'm in shock someone stole my cattle. Dad never had a problem, and I haven't heard of anything like this happening around here."

Luke sat in the chair across from her. "They might have thought the place would be an easy target without Owen. Listen, it's not your fault. Tomorrow we'll fix the fence, and I'll go into town and ask around."

She opened her mouth and he cut her off. "You know as well as I some of those ranchers are hardcore, and they don't like dealing with women."

"Sad, but true," she said with a heavy sigh. "They had one of their gala dinners and didn't invite, me and I don't think it's because I'm in mourning."

The misery in her eyes and the frown on her face bothered him, but he knew from experience, mourning was a deeply personal thing and it could not be fixed quickly.

"Now what about Greg Sparks? You trust him to be foreman?"

"Yes, I do."

"Good you need someone you have faith in. Why don't we get some sleep and talk with Greg in the morning to work out a plan to keep this place secure?"

"Luke? Thank you for having my back." She gave him a small smile.

Warmth zinged through his body. "Well I'm tired, I'm going to bed."

He stood and walked to his room, feeling her gaze upon him the whole while.

Later in bed, he wondered if he would ever get his wish of Meg loving him back. There was so much going on and he didn't want her to mistake loving him for needing him. It was a very long time before sleep finally came.

The next day, Meg sat on the front porch taking a much-needed break. She had worked out a schedule with Greg for guarding the ranch, and they both agreed they needed to hire a few more men. It still outraged her that the sheriff would only take her statement over the phone. Of course, dead women trumped cattle rustling any day, but couldn't he have spared a man to look at the crime scene?

Sitting back against the old rocking chair, she tapped her fingernails on its scarred arm. And there was Luke and the comfort he'd given her. Her eyes closed as she relived their embrace and almost kiss. The tenderness and sweetness of it haunted her, and tears filled her eyes as she wished for her father. The torment in her heart never subsided, if anything it grew.

A huge sigh escaped her when she saw Detective Timbers' car drive up to the house. *What now?* It sure wasn't about her cattle, and she couldn't stand to hear more bad news. Her whole body stiffened as he got out of the car and walked up the porch steps.

"Morning, I'd like to talk to you." The look in his eyes gave the impression he knew something, and it made her uneasy.

"Finally. I'm surprised they sent you but missing cattle is serious business."

He didn't acknowledge her comment; instead, he sat down and took a small notebook out of his jacket pocket. "How well do you know Harry Kelly?"

The question threw her—she thought for sure he was going after Luke. "All my life. We weren't close neighbors, but I saw him occasionally. Why?"

Timbers scribbled something down in his notebook before he glanced up at her with his beady, brown eyes. "He did own the property, and from all my research, he wasn't a very likable man. He beat his wife and kids. Now, if everyone knew about his abuse, why didn't anyone stop him? Your father should have done something."

The urge to slap him overwhelmed her. Standing up, she stared at him. "Well, that's all the time I have for today. If you'll excuse me I have cattle to find."

"No, I'm not done with you."

"Oh, I think you are. In case you haven't heard, my father just died, someone stole my cattle, and there are dead people on land I now own. I think I have more than enough on my plate. If you're not here to take a statement about my cattle I'm asking you to leave."

His nostrils flared and his lips flattened into a grim line. "I'll ignore your little tirade, you are in mourning as you say, but I will be back and I will get answers to my questions. I wonder what the townspeople will think once they've heard you're being uncooperative." He stood, put his notebook back into his pocket and went back to his car.

Shocked, she sank back down into the chair, her heart raced and her jaw dropped open. *What the hell?*

Luke tramped through the dense woods looking for the old, abandoned cabin he and David used to hide in. Ever since he'd talked to his father, he'd had an urgent need to see it.

The nursing home was pleasant enough. It had been hard to see his father so withered in a wheelchair, and he'd had a hard time looking the old bastard in the eye. There was never any love between them.

Luke shook his head, remembering. He still couldn't figure how he'd been so wrong about his brother. According to his dad, David had killed those women and probably many more, hence the reason his father had killed him. The brother he had known would never be capable of killing anyone, but life was so crazy and turned around, he didn't know what to believe anymore.

The century-old dwelling came into sight, and he stopped, staring at it. They'd planned futures together without their old man. It had been their secret refuge, but somehow his father knew about it. He had said the evidence of David's insanity was in the cabin, and now Luke hesitated to enter.

Slowly, he walked to the door and pushed it open. It was dark and smelled of dampness. Leaving the door open, he located the oil lamp on the table near the door and lit it. There were two windows in the place, but they had been long ago boarded up.

The log cabin only had one room. The history he always imagined intrigued him, but today he wasn't here to imagine, he was here to find the truth. It'd been about eight years since he'd been there, and a few things had been added. A couple chairs and a decent sized kitchen table sat in the middle of the room. Luke's stomach roiled at the possibilities.

Taking the oil lamp, he brought it to the big table and immediately felt the blood drain from his face. There were pictures, many pictures of women— some alive and some dead. A loud noise of distress came from his throat and he closed his eyes. *Why? How?*

Finally, he picked up some of the photos and examined them. They were before and after shots of too many women. The before pictures showed a relaxed smiling female and the after, they'd clearly been beaten to death. Slumping down into a chair, he put his head in his hands and swore.

David? How could he have done these things? Sitting up he glanced around the cabin remembering how David had played doctor, trying to undo the destruction their father had left. Cuts, bruises, a broken arm— David took care of them. Perhaps the constant beatings had made him a killer. It was too hard to reconcile. He needed to go to the police; there were a whole lot of pictures, and a whole lot of bodies yet to be found.

Deciding to leave the cabin as he found it, he blew out the lamp and put it back on the table near the door. He closed the door and traipsed back through the woods, got into his truck and drove into town.

Luke sat in the truck staring at the police station door. The last thing he wanted to do was drag his brother's name through the mud, and there was still the little problem of David's body. He didn't want any blame shifted on him. His shoulders tensed as he got out of the truck. Truth time.

As soon as he walked in, he immediately honed in on Detective Timbers, who was smirking at him. "Detective." He nodded and took off his hat. "I might have some info you need."

Timbers stood up and somehow he looked more authoritative than usual. If he was trying to be imposing, he was doing a damn good job. "Coffee?"

"No, I'm fine. I just want to tell you what I know and leave."

"Of course, follow me we can talk in this room." He opened the door that bore the words INTERROGATION ROOM in black, blocked letters. "Sit."

Damn, Timbers made him feel like a suspect, and he didn't like it one bit. Not one little, tiny bit. But he sat in the chair and waited.

Timbers took a digital recorder out of his pocket, placed it on the table between them and turned it on.

"You are here of your own free will?"

"Yes."

"Please state your name for the record."

"Luke Kelly."

"Not Lucas?"

"No, Luke."

"I'm led to understand you have a confession to make."

Luke's eyes widened. "No, no confession. You must be thinking of someone else. I came here to share what information I have in the case of the dead women."

"Sure, go ahead. Where did you meet these women?"

"Damn, if you aren't mule headed. I found evidence on the property in a cabin no one but David and I knew about."

"So you're the only one around who knew of this place?"

Luke shook his head. "I have to amend my last statement. My father knew about it, too."

"I see. What is in this cabin?"

"Pictures of women, alive and dead. Many pictures. I hadn't been there for years but someone moved a table and chairs into it. It's a small rundown place. I hate to have to say this, but I think David might have had something to do with all this."

"You think or you know?"

"I have no smoking gun if that's what you mean, but my father thinks it's David too."

Timbers laughed. "You're father doesn't even know what year it is. His words mean nothing, absolutely nothing. So let me get this straight. Your father told you about the cabin and David recently. To top it off, you expect me to believe you?"

Luke clenched and unclenched his hands. This is not what he had planned. Now Timbers thought him guilty. *How did everything get so turned around?* "Believe what you want, I just thought I'd give you the info I had, but if you're not interested, fine."

"I never said I wasn't interested. I just wanted to test the waters. I'll need you to take me to the cabin. I suppose your fingerprints are all over it."

Luke offered a grimace of regret. "Yes, they are."

Timbers shook his head. "Your fingerprints, but it wasn't you?"

"I was just there to look around, and I touched everything. You'll probably find other prints besides mine. My father knew about the place, and of course David's would still be there."

Timbers stared at Luke until he felt as though his throat was closing. Rubbing his neck, the sensation finally went away but the anxiety of being a suspect remained.

"So, tell me, Luke, where is David?"

"I don't know."

"You're lying. You know, Luke, I've been a cop for a long time, and I know these things."

Luke's shoulders relaxed, and he had to hold back a smile. Timbers wasn't old enough to have been a cop for a long time. It was all a show with this guy. He didn't know a thing, and he wasn't going to know anything else.

Timbers cleared his throat. "I'll give Miss O'Brien a call and ask if we can search the cabin. I still think you have something to do with the murders. Nothing gets by me."

Damn. He didn't want Meg involved. It hadn't occurred to him the cabin was on her property. This whole thing was a mess, and now he was sorry he'd opened his mouth. Good thing he hadn't mentioned that David was dead or they'd have strung him up already.

Timbers stepped out into the hall for a minute and then came back in. "Miss O'Brien is on her way. She didn't even know there was a cabin, but she gave her okay, and men are heading up there now to search it."

"Well, I'll go out front and wait for Meg."

"Sit down. You are my prime suspect or person of interest. I hate that term, person of interest, people aren't stupid they know it means suspect, at least it does to me."

Luke opened his mouth but no words came out. "Suspect? I'm the one who told you about the cabin," he protested.

Timbers laughed. "Damn, you don't know nothin' do you? The real perpetrator always inserts himself into the case."

Luke's eyes narrowed. "Just how long have you been a detective?"

Timbers threw back his shoulders. "Almost a year now. I was working in the next county, but I'm needed here for this investigation. I guess you don't get many murder cases here, and the sheriff called for reinforcements."

"How lucky for the sheriff you were free." Luke sneered. He wanted to close his eyes, but he couldn't remember if not-guilty people slept or if it was the guilty ones who took naps in the interrogation room. He'd better not chance it. He sat back in the chair, his arms crossed, trying to appear innocent.

"You know you could just confess and save your town the cost of a lengthy trial."

Luke almost laughed. He wasn't much of a TV watcher but he knew he'd heard those words on some cop show. "I guess those words would interest me if I was guilty, but you'll have to save them for some other person of interest."

The door opened, and Meg stood there, distress written all over her face. "Luke?"

Meg's heart pounded so hard she could hear it thumping in her chest as she stared at Luke. Detective Timbers had said Luke confessed, and for the life of her, she couldn't understand it. Luke a killer? A serial killer? Nevertheless, there he was in the interrogation room. Her heart dropped watching Luke frown and Timbers gloat.

"I didn't know about the cabin. I never ventured that far into the woods in that section of the property. Have they arrested you yet?"

Luke shook his head, and his eyes pleaded for understanding.

She hardened her heart and looked away. "Now what?" she asked Timbers.

"We have our best guys gathering the evidence now but just his fingerprints being there is enough for me. I'm going to arrest him. Are you sure you don't know anything? I know you two were close."

"I never knew…" She took a deep shaky breath. "I'm having a hard time believing the whole thing."

"Then don't," Luke said.

Glancing at him, she wanted to cry. He looked so hurt and angry. He probably expected her to come to his defense but she just didn't know. The flicker of raw pain in his eyes changed her mind— he wasn't a killer.

"Fingerprints don't mean a thing. All it proves is he was there, which, from what I understand is why he came here, to tell you about the cabin. Why would he tell you if he was the killer? Makes no kind of sense to me. I've known Luke all my life, and we've had our ups and downs, but he couldn't and wouldn't hurt a woman."

Timbers smiled at her. "Good thing what you happen to think doesn't matter. I appreciate you giving us permission to search the cabin."

"I'd like to talk to Meg alone," Luke requested.

Timbers laughed. "So you two can cook up a few alibis? I don't think so."

"I want a lawyer."

Timbers gave Luke a look of disgust. "Fine, Miss O'Brien, I need you to leave."

"I'll call a friend of my dad's. He'll be here in no time, Luke."

Luke nodded. "Thanks for believing in me." He gave her a worried smile.

"You're a good man, Luke Kelly, and don't you forget it." She shot him what she hoped was a reassuring smile, ashamed she had doubted him for a single second.

"Just give me the name of the lawyer, and I'd be happy to call him," Timbers offered.

She laughed at him and left the room. He'd never make the phone call. There was something off with that arrogant man. She wished she'd looked at the cabin before granting permission to have it searched. All she wanted was to have the murderer caught and then maybe she could work on getting closer to Luke. She wanted him to stay with her, to love her and perhaps marry her.

Later that night, the house was quiet, too quiet. Loneliness poured over her as she tried to catch up on the dreaded paperwork. Her father had a head for numbers, not her, but it had to be done. The computer screen glowed as though it waited for her input, but with Luke in jail, she couldn't concentrate.

Her lawyer, Bates Barker, indicated it didn't look good, but he was sure he'd get Luke home by tomorrow. He also asked her many questions about Luke's dad. Her best bet, it was David who killed those women and left. They should be searching for similar crimes in different parts of the country. Poor Luke.

As she drummed her fingers on the big, wooden desk, she became convinced she needed to find David. Doing an internet search, she typed David Kelly into the search bar and gasped when she saw there were almost six thousand people named David Kelly. Putting in more search words narrowed it down to five hundred, but that was still too many people to wade through. How could there be so many?

A cup of coffee sounded good, and she got up and went into the kitchen to pour herself a cup. Why had David left? No one ever had a good reason. He'd just disappeared around the same time Luke had, and she couldn't ask Mr. Kelly; he always called her a whore when he saw her.

Back at the computer, she put in David's date of birth and while no one came up with the exact date, there were one hundred and two people with the same birth year. The coffee didn't help in giving her a second wind, but she needed to push on. She was afraid if she stopped, she'd lose her search. There was a possibility he never left Texas; after all, he loved ranching. Her list ended with sixteen names, and she found phone numbers for all but five of them.

Glancing at the clock, she frowned. It was too late to make calls. It would have to wait until the morning. She printed out her information, turned off the computer and walked into the kitchen. The rest of the coffee she poured down the sink, and then she started toward her bedroom. What if she found David? Maybe it wasn't such a good idea, if he was a killer and all.

The house was too quiet, and she couldn't remember a time it had been like this. If only her father was here to guide her and to help Luke. Heck, Luke might even be mad she considered David a suspect, but who else was there? Good gravy, it looked like she'd have to go and see Mr. Kelly after all. Just because he was old didn't mean *he* hadn't committed the murders. She shook her head; she'd go in the morning to see that ornery old cuss. She'd do it for Luke's sake.

The lack of sleep put her in a bad mood, and seeing Harry Kelly wasn't going to improve it any. Meg sat in her truck in the nursing home parking lot trying to get up enough energy for what was bound to be a nasty visit. At least she finally knew why he hated her so much. She'd hate too if her spouse had made a child with another. So many secrets for so many years.

Closing her eyes, she shook her head, took a deep breath and unfastened her seatbelt. She said a quick prayer for peace, opened her eyes, and got out of the truck. It seemed like a nice place with many different flowers blooming and a great big gazebo off to one side. She pulled her shoulders back and steeled herself.

The receptionist was a warm friendly woman with gray hair. She smiled and told Meg in what room she could find Mr. Kelly. Meg walked down the long hallway. The acrid menthol smell of Ben-Gay assaulted her. Her father had used enough of it, and she knew the scent well. She felt a flash of sorrow.

A gruff "Come in," answered her knock. She opened the door and stepped inside. Harry was an older, thinner version of himself, and she hoped he'd remember her.

"I've been waiting for you to come see me. Heard tell your daddy is dead. Can't say I'll miss him. After all, he did ruin my family." He gave her a long hard stare. "Guess you already know about your daddy and my wife, but do you know about David?" He studied her again and nodded. "It's good you finally know."

"The truth is always best."

"Especially when evil deeds come to light. I could hardly bear to live with my wife anymore after your father had her. She was nothing but a damn whore, and I had to raise a bastard. She never stepped out on me again, I can tell you that."

His anger filled the small room, and for a moment, she forgot what she wanted to say. Walking to the window, she panned the view, trying to get her bearings. Finally, she turned back and met his stare. "Do you know where David is?"

"What's it to you?"

"Luke's in jail. They believe he killed the women found on the property you used to own."

"The property you now own?" He smirked and shrugged his shoulders. "Luke's no killer, they'll see that soon enough. He doesn't have the backbone for killin'."

"They have their minds made up, and I wanted to talk to David and see if he knew anything."

He laughed. "David ain't never coming back, so you'd better get your ass out of here and find someone else to blame. And don't you even look in my direction. I'm a lover not a fighter."

Her jaw dropped. Not a fighter? Who was he kidding? And for someone who supposedly didn't even know his name he was extremely sharp. Had Luke lied to her?

The sheriff wouldn't allow her to see Luke again, and his lawyer told her not to expect him home anytime soon. At least for the next seventy-two hours. So much for promising to get him home by tonight. Three more bodies had turned up, and the police wanted to get the case wrapped up as soon as possible.

Yawning, she rubbed the back of her neck, feeling the tightness of her muscles. Her whole body was tense. What she wouldn't give for one of those fancy massages.

There'd be no extras in the near future. How much would Luke's defense cost? What if he was found guilty? It happened all the time, and the wrong person went to jail. Harry knew more than he was letting on; he had to. How did he know David wouldn't be coming back, and what was all that bull about being a lover, not a fighter? He had smacked his whole family around for years.

Her headache worsened, and she loosened her braid, letting her hair hang down her back. Massaging her scalp, she entered the office. Finding David was imperative, but where to start? Even after narrowing down her search, there were many David Kellys.

Grabbing the phone, she began to call nine of the Kellys with phone numbers. After the first few numbers, she became discouraged, and by the end of the list, things appeared hopeless. There were still six more on her short list and after paying an online service, she downloaded the addresses for them all.

Her jaw dropped when she continued to read the information on the computer. It had a section for who each person might be related to. One had Harry's name listed. Her heart beat so hard, it surprised her she couldn't hear it. This had to be the one, and he didn't live very far from them. If it was him, why didn't he stay in contact with his family? Surely, he knew about the bodies being found.

Oh hell, she hoped he hadn't up and moved. He was her number one suspect, and she needed to find him and make sure he didn't go anywhere. If he was innocent, he'd have stepped forward before now. Sighing, she got up and turned the lights out as she walked out into the hallway. A loud bang from the kitchen startled her, and she froze. What had that been? A thud was followed by a muffled curse. Her blood pumped faster, her breaths came in little gasps.

One step at a time, she slowly made her way toward the kitchen. Stopping at the end of the hall, she had a good view but didn't see anyone. Not sure what to do, she walked into the kitchen, and she spotted someone sitting in the living room.

It was David.

Kathleen Ball

Chapter Five

David turned and gave her a weary grin. He had the same dark hair and blue eyes as Luke, but where Luke was muscular, David appeared thin. "Hope I didn't scare you. I heard about the arrest and got here as soon as I could."

Floored, she stared at him. "Where have you been?"

David reached inside the tall cabinet and grabbed a bottle of whiskey. He took out a glass, splashed some whiskey in it and cocked his brow at her.

"No, you go ahead." She watched him put the whiskey away. He didn't act guilty, but what did guilty look like?

"I've been drifting mostly. I finally bought a small place not too far from here. I don't get much of a chance to keep up with current events, but I saw Luke's picture on the television at the diner this morning. He's innocent, you know."

"I know."

"The bodies were found on our land? I don't understand any of this."

"Technically, the land belongs to me. My dad bought it to keep it for you and Luke."

David sighed, sat down on the wooden chair and sipped his drink. "Where is your dad?"

A part of her heart sliced away. "He died recently. I'm still reeling from his death, and now with Luke in jail, well, it's been hard."

He nodded and stared at her as though he was taking her measure. "You know."

"That you're my brother? Yes, I know."

"Hell of a thing. My ma and your dad ruined so many lives. That crazy son of a bitch smacked us all around. He used to call me the bastard, and when he told me to leave and never come back, I left." He dragged his hand over his face. "How do we get Luke out of jail?"

Pulling out a chair, she sat. "The lawyer thinks he'll be released in the morning, but there is a detective on the case who is convinced Luke is the murderer. There is a cabin-"

"We used to play there and hide from Dad."

Meg nodded. "There are pictures of the women who were murdered there."

"Damn. When did Harry die?"

She blinked at him and furrowed her brow. "He's alive and lives at the nursing home in town."

"Have the police talked to him? He's dangerous."

"You think Harry is responsible? It could have been someone else who used your land as a burial site. In fact, you were on my short list of suspects."

He leaned forward and put his elbows on the kitchen table. "Not anymore?"

"Yes,—no—dang, I don't know what I'm saying anymore. I wouldn't expect you to come here to help Luke if you were a serial killer."

David swigged down the last of the whiskey. "Well, I'll be back in the morning." He stood and picked up the hat that he'd left on the counter.

"Where are you staying?"

"The old homestead, unless you object."

"No, I don't own the house. Your father sold it to a nice family. You might as well stay here."

He rubbed the back of his neck. "Thank you. I'll take you up on your offer. I'll get my bag out of my truck."

She watched him walk out of the house, hoping she hadn't made a mistake.

Luke leaned the back of his head against the brick wall. There was no way he'd allow himself to sleep. Six other men shared the cell with him, and he didn't like the look of any of them. He didn't even know where the sheriff had rounded them up from because he was certain he'd never seen them before. A crime wave in a small town, go figure.

The other men didn't have trouble sleeping in the holding cell, and each of them snored. When was his luck going to change? He'd had near about all he could take the last few years. Meg was the one good thing, her and his mustangs.

He shook his head, thinking about how Meg rescued and trained the mustangs. He'd hurt her by leaving. Heck, any other woman would have sold the horses to spite him but not his Meg. He whispered aloud, "My Meg." It had a nice sound to it and it warmed him.

Damn his father. Damn David too. David had killed the women, his father had killed David, and he had helped bury David. It didn't even sound plausible to him, and he was sure the detective would say the same thing. Maybe he should confess to burying David. He ran his hand over his face. There was no way to win. Some people weren't meant to be winners, and he was one of them. As soon as they found David's body, it would tighten the noose already around his neck.

He planned on a future with Meg. She might not know it yet, but that was his plan. He loved her, and now it wouldn't be right to tell her. What was the jail time for someone who helped his father bury his brother? He was sure to be fried if they convicted him of those murders. There was no way he was going to ask Meg to stand by him. It would ruin her chance for any happiness.

Closing his eyes, he took a deep breath and slowly let it escape. Thinking about her with another man put a lump in his throat. She deserved a husband and children, lots of children who looked just like her. He opened his eyes as he heard the guards changing shifts. It must be morning. He wasn't sure if he should feel glad it was a new day or not.

The other men began to rouse, each griping about having to sleep in a holding cell. They all knew each other, and they kept eyeing him. Trying to avoid all eye contact, he stared at the filthy cement floor. He'd have to make a clean break with Meg and tell her to get out of his life. It was the only way, and hopefully she'd get riled enough to walk away and never look back.

Meg crossed and uncrossed her legs trying to get comfortable on the cool metal chair in the waiting room at the police station. If ever a time she needed her dad, it was now. Both Luke and David were in interrogation rooms without lawyers.

As soon as she and David walked into the station, Detective Timbers had grabbed David saying he was wanted for questioning. What a mess, and if she'd been thinking halfway straight she'd have left David home.

David was nice enough, much quieter than she remembered. Something haunted him. She could see it in his eyes. Luke hadn't been informed David was back in town. Meg wanted to be the one to tell him the good news, but now she didn't know if it was good news or not. She'd called the only other defense attorney in town, Jed Hanks. It was just her luck he was out fishing, but his wife said she'd send him over when he got back and she hoped he caught enough fish for dinner.

She shifted again on the hard chair. Finally, a door opened, and Luke came out looking weary. When he saw her, his eyes lit up but only for a second. She could feel a thick wall suddenly fall between them and it left her chilled.

He nodded at her and went out the door.

Meg quickly followed. "Luke? Luke wait."

He stopped and waited, not turning around to look at her.

"Luke, David is back. Did they tell you? They have him in another interrogation room."

He stared at her, his brow furrowed. Then all color left his face. "David? My brother? How is that possible? Did you see him?" He grabbed her shoulders and stared at her as though he'd never seen her before. "Did you see him?"

"Yes, let go you're hurting me."

He released her. "Sorry."

"He came to the house. He saw the murders on TV and came to find out what was going on."

He closed his eyes and took a deep breath. "I don't know who came to the house, but it wasn't David. It's not possible. How? Who? What is going on?" He opened his eyes and stared at her.

She reached out to touch his arm but he flinched away. "You're father told him to leave and not come back, I guess."

"You're sure it's him? Has he changed at all?"

"I don't know where you're going with all this. Of course, it's him! You're acting like you don't want him here."

"I can't talk about it here. Let's get in the truck."

She nodded and pulled her keys out of her pocket. They walked to the truck in silence and he didn't open her door for her. Something was very wrong. They both got in and closed the doors. "What is going on?" Her voice was higher pitched than usual.

Luke ran his hands through his hair making it stand on end. He glanced at her and glanced away.

"Luke, look at me."

He turned his body facing toward her with his back against the door and she wanted to cry at the confusion and pain in his eyes. "Meg, David is dead."

"Why would you think him dead? I know he's been gone, but you were gone, too." She stared straight ahead at the road as she drove.

Luke heard her but didn't know what to say. He stared at the countryside. Swallowing hard, he wondered what to tell her. He couldn't tell her he knew David was dead, because he'd helped bury him. There was no way the man was David. His head began to ache, and he closed his eyes. He had a sinking feeling it was really David. Meg knew what he looked like. If he hadn't helped to bury David, then who?

He wanted to throw up. The most likely person was the girl who was in the grave he thought they'd buried David in. He never checked to see who he was burying. His father was the key. Maybe David left after he found the body and used him to help him get rid of the evidence.

"Where is David staying?" He gazed at her pretty profile wishing he hadn't brought all this on her.

"With us of course. I can't wait until you see him. I'm so excited. I bet Timbers doesn't keep him long. He might be home before dinner." She turned and smiled. "You don't look so good."

"I guess being at the police station didn't agree with me."

"Of, course." She turned into the drive and parked near the house. "If you want to take a nap, it's fine with me."

Nodding he gave her a small smile. His heart ached. He loved her, but he couldn't have her not now, not ever.

They got out of the truck and walked to the house. Meg grabbed his hand and held on to it. It felt so right but he knew it to be wrong. "A nap sounds good, I'm beat."

"Sure, you go on. I'll figure out what's for dinner."

The concern in her voice crushed him. He didn't deserve her. Without a word, he went to his room and closed the door. He took a deep breath and stood in front of the window. The only thing he knew for certain was he wasn't the killer. If he came clean, they'd blame the whole of it on him, and he'd never see the light of day again.

The door opened, but he didn't turn around. He heard her walk toward him. She snaked her arm around his waist and pressed herself against his back. "I believe in you, Luke." Her voice was low and husky.

His body reacted to her nearness and a shudder went through him. Turning, he crushed her to him, holding her tight. He let go and cupped her face in his hands. Her blue eyes held promises of a future and he told himself to walk away but he couldn't. "I love you with everything inside me."

Her eyes teared. "I love you too, Luke. Now is the time for us to lean on each other. Please don't push me away."

He knew he'd go to hell but he couldn't help it. He lowered his head and claimed her mouth.

Her cherry lips were so soft under his, and when she opened her mouth to him, he groaned. Maybe he should stop, but maybe this is all he'll ever have. "God, you're beautiful," he whispered against her lips. A blush started at her neck, and he wondered if her whole body was rosy red.

He kissed her throat and loved the resulting shiver. Pulling back, he looked into her passion filled eyes before he started to unbutton her shirt. He kissed each bit of skin as he exposed it. Her bra was lacy and red, and he wanted to laugh. He'd have thought she'd have on a practical white one. She was the ranch owner and the foreman before that. It was nice to know she wasn't colorless anymore.

"Did I mention you're beautiful?" Her whole body was a light shade of red.

He started at her feet, kissing them and she squirmed.

"My feet are ticklish"

"I noticed."

"Mmmm. You're making me crazy."

"That's my intent."

He lay next to her and stroked her hair. "Ready?"

Looking into his eyes, she nodded.

He kissed her deeply. He moved against her and couldn't believe how good it felt. Heaven was here with Meg. Her eyes were closed and she breathed deeply. "I didn't know. I mean I've read about it being good, but I tried it and figured it wasn't for me."

"Meg, you were made for loving. You are so responsive and we fit together perfectly."

She opened her eyes and a serene smile crossed her face. "We do, don't we? My body is so alive, it tingles."

"Tingling is always good and so is kissing."

Before she could respond the sound of a vehicle driving up startled them. "It's probably David."

Luke gave her a quick kiss and jumped out of bed, getting dressed as fast as he could. The fact David was alive still boggled his mind. "I'll meet you out there."

She nodded as she reached for her shirt. "I'll catch up."

He barely nodded and was quickly out the door. The man standing before him was definitely David and he couldn't believe what he was seeing. His brother was alive.

David took a step toward him and they met in the middle embracing each other. It was all a lie, everything his father told him was a big lie.

"Good to see you, brother. I figured I'd never see you again." David's voice sounded scratchy and full of emotion.

Luke swallowed hard in disbelief. "I was led to believe you were dead. It's a miracle you're here."

"Not a miracle. The old man told me to leave and never come back." He shrugged and looked away. "I abided his wishes. Then I heard you lit out, and I had no reason to come back before now."

Luke nodded. "My wife and daughter died, and I was in bad shape so I came here. Owen was always a very generous man." They went inside, and he put the coffee on. "Dad pretty much ran me off the same night."

David turned a kitchen chair around and straddled it. "Wife and daughter? Oh God, I'm so sorry."

"It was a car accident, and I was more than banged up. Owen insisted I come here to heal."

"Somehow I always thought you and Meg would be together."

"I love her, never stopped. We're finding our way."

David nodded. "Things have changed since I was in town last. Who the hell is this Timbers guy, and why does he have a hard on for me?"

"You? I thought he was making a case against me."

"Perfect loose cannon. He told me about the bodies. I never knew they were there."

"All sixteen of them. I can't fathom it." Luke shook his head. "Do you think Mom knew?"

"Knew what?" David asked. His brow furrowed.

Luke poured coffee for both of them and handed David a mug. He sat at the table across from him. "Did she know anything about the bodies? I hate to say this, but Dad may be involved."

David shrugged his shoulders. "We'll never know, and with dad having Alzheimer's—"

"He's as sharp as ever," Luke said cringing " He's pulling this whole not knowing anything to keep from being a suspect. He was lucid when I talked to him."

"He always was a mean son of a bitch, and he hated me. His damn hatred ran deep. I often wished he'd just kill Owen and leave me alone."

"Well, Mom never had a moment's peace either. He was a hateful, evil man, and I'm wondering if he had anything to do with the murders."

A feral smile crept over David's face. "Maybe I can make him mad enough to confess."

Meg was glad Luke and David were able to see each other, but she wished to be back in bed with Luke. Her body hummed, and her smile wouldn't quit. He loved her. Butterflies filled her stomach as she replayed the memory of his words.

It had felt so right making love with him. They were finally on the right track, and nothing was going to get in their way. Too much wasted time had gone by already.

However, she had a lot of work to do. The ranch wasn't going to run itself.

She waltzed outside, and Luke held out his hand for her to grab. They shared a loving glance as they laced their fingers together.

"I'm glad you two finally got together. I can't believe you're both here," said David softly. "My brother and sister are in love. Good Lord, it's weird to say." He laughed. "I want to go out to the corner property and see where all the bodies were buried. I still can't believe it."

"Sure I'll take you." Luke fished the keys to the truck out of his front pocket. "You coming?" He yanked her hand until she was leaning on him. Then he leaned down and kissed her, leaving her breathless.

"Yes."

They piled into the truck, and David asked many questions about the ranch. She answered them all.

"I have to tell you, I'm impressed, Meg. Your knowledge of the ranch is astounding."

She shrugged. "Not really. I was the foreman before daddy died. I don't know your property as well as mine, but I'm learning. I run the mustangs on your ranch and a few head of cattle too."

"You own the whole thing?"

She felt him stiffen beside her. "David, Dad bought it to hold for the two of you. As soon as everything is settled I'll deed it over to you both."

"How much did your dad pay for the ranch?"

She shook her head. "You know I never gave it much thought. I can look it up when we get back home."

"I was just wondering what Harry did with the money."

"I assumed he pays for the nursing home with it," Luke said.

"Still, the land is worth millions," David insisted.

"What it's worth and what was paid must be two entirely different numbers. My dad didn't have that kind of money. Don't worry, I won't make you buy your land back. It'll be yours free and clear."

David gave her a quick nod and turned his head, looking out the window.

Frowning, she glanced at Luke who frowned back.

"Meg was able to save the mustangs," Luke said, breaking the awkward silence.

"How much did you pay for them?"

"David, what is your problem?" Luke demanded.

"I'm just thinking maybe they took advantage of Harry and his Alzheimer's."

Meg gasped. "First of all I paid for the mustangs myself after your dad shot one of them in the head. Second, Harry is as sharp as a tack. His memory problems started the day the bodies were found. Do things seem suspicious? Yes they do, but not on my or my dad's part."

David still stared out the window. "I can see the police tape."

"It's so sad. Look at all the land they've dug up. I really hope there are no more bodies out there." Meg sighed as she shook her head.

Luke stopped the truck and they all got out and stared.

"How many bodies did you say were found?" David asked as he took in the excavated land.

"Sixteen, I believe was the last count." Luke rubbed the back of his neck.

David pointed to the horses in the distance. "The mustangs? Is the stallion in the front Poseidon?"

She shook her head. "No, your dad shot Poseidon. I bought the horses after that. I've managed to double the herd."

"Meg is a great horse trainer." Luke smiled at her.

"I bet they're worth a pretty penny. I guess I can rent you the land you keep them on. Once the land is handed over I mean." David walked closer to the gravesites.

She put her hand on Luke's arm. "What is with him and all the money talk? He makes me feel like I stole the horses and my dad stole the land from your dad."

Luke shrugged. "I don't know, but I don't like it either. Don't sign anything over to us just yet. I want to be sure of his intent. I don't plan to be blindsided by David trying to sell his half or something."

"Smart idea."

He leaned down and kissed her cheek. "I had the most amazing time with you."

It suddenly felt hotter than usual. "Me too," she said as she ducked her head and walked toward David. Amazing was a good word for it. Actually, it had been better than amazing. He proved her conclusion sex was overrated to be false.

"Are you sure they only found sixteen? I would have thought they'd find more."

Her brow furrowed. "Why do you think that?"

He kept staring at the holes in the ground. "How'd they find the first one?"

Luke caught up to them and took her hand in his. "Owen had an offer for this parcel of land. He thought with the sale I'd be able to buy cattle and build a new house."

"You agreed? That doesn't sound like you, Luke. You loved this land."

"No, I told him no." Luke shrugged.

David's eyes grew wider. "If you told him no, then why is it all torn up?" He stared at her. "He never intended to give us back the land. What came with the land? You? Maybe he thought it the only way to get you married."

She stiffened and gasped. "I wasn't looking to get married. I don't know what your problem is or what you're insinuating, but my father was a fine man."

"A paragon of virtue." He sneered.

Luke took a step toward David. "Lay off. I don't know what you're problem is, but I expect you to treat Meg with respect."

But David didn't respond. Instead, he walked the perimeter of the police tape staring at the dirt.

"My brother is an ass." Luke shook his head. "Talk about a bitter disposition."

Meg laced her fingers with his. "He's changed, but who knows what he's been through the last few years."

Luke gave her hand a squeeze. "I'm happy to see him. Honestly, I thought he was dead. It's a miracle he's here, but he needs to filter his thoughts."

She reached up and stroked the side of his face. He hadn't shaved, and his day's growth looked downright sexy on him. "He probably needs time."

"I guess. Look at him. He's examining each grave. I don't know but there's something not quite right. I can see from here all the holes in the ground."

"It's all new to him." She wasn't sure she believed her own words. David seemed fascinated as he walked around. "Are we still planning to sell half of the mustangs?"

"I haven't even had time to think about it."

"You're welcome to stay at the house for as long as you like."

Leaning over, he kissed her cheek. "Thank you, but it wouldn't be right to take advantage of your new position as owner. Until the land is transferred over, I think we should sit tight and wait. You might not be allowed to transfer a crime scene." He nodded at David who ended his examination of the property.

"You're moving out?" She furrowed her brow. The house was empty enough without her dad in it.

"I'm just thinking out loud. I could go and stay in the bunkhouse."

"You can do what you want, little brother, but Meg asked me to stay and I'm planning on it." David made a point of staring at their clasped hands and then looked at Luke with his right eyebrow cocked.

"Of course Luke is staying. Are we done here? I have paperwork to look over and I need to meet with my foreman."

"Who is the foreman these days? I heard you had the job. I'm a bit surprised Owen let you play foreman."

She stiffened. "I earned the job. Nothing was handed to me. My new foreman is Greg Sparks. You might remember him."

David laughed. "If things had been different, I'd be owner and you'd be living off my charity."

"David, leave it alone," Luke warned.

"Sorry, I just keep thinking how different my life would have been if Owen had manned up and claimed me as his. Instead, I was sentenced to a life of hell."

Tears filled her eyes. "Don't talk about my father that way. To me, he was a kind, loving person."

David snorted. "You got all the breaks didn't you?"

Luke dropped Meg's hand and walked to David until they were toe-to-toe and eye-to-eye. "Listen, lay off. I know you had it hard, I was there. Meg is innocent of all sins you believe her father did. It doesn't help for your bitterness to overflow into her life. If you'd rather find somewhere else to live you are more than welcome to. If you plan to stay at the house, you'd better apologize and adjust your attitude."

David stared at Luke for a long moment and then shrugged. "Sure." He turned and nodded at Meg. "Sorry."

All three of them piled into the truck, Luke behind the wheel, with Meg in the middle, and he held her small work-worn hand in his. He gave it a slight squeeze and turned his head, offering a reassuring smile. It felt right to have her next to him, and he hoped it would be forever. They'd had five years stolen from them, and he didn't want to wait any longer, but his words could wait until they were alone.

She leaned her head on his shoulder and sighed. It was a sigh of contentment. Too bad his brother was being an ass. There was so much he needed to sort out. Two things were clear: his father was a killer, and he'd helped him bury one of his victims. Luke's stomach roiled, his body tensed. Meg lifted her head and gave him a questioning glance. He smiled back at her.

"Is something wrong?" She rubbed her other hand up and down his arm.

"Nothing a little time alone with you won't cure."

On the other side of Meg, David groaned. "Oh please. Luke, you sound like a calf searching for its ma. You aren't making a play for her to get your hands on her ranch are you?"

Gravel crunched beneath tires as Luke pulled the truck to the side of the road. "Get out."

"What's your problem?" David gave him a cold look.

"My problem?" Luke twisted in his seat to stare at his brother. "I guess it's how suspicious you are of everything. If you wanted to be involved in all decisions, you should never have left. I don't like you badgering Meg with all your questions about money. You make it seem as though she's done something wrong. Now, get out!"

David frowned, and his eyes narrowed. "Whatever you say, little brother. Meg should be worried. Didn't you marry before hoping to get the ranch?"

Meg squeezed his arm keeping him from getting out of the truck and pounding on David.

David opened the door, got out, and slammed the door. The truck tires spun as Luke drove away.

"Why is he acting like such a jerk, Luke? I feel as though I'm missing something. Do you think he expected my dad to give him part of my ranch?"

He shook his head. "You got me. I don't like the way he talks to you, and I'm putting an end to it. It might be better if he found another place to live or better yet if he went back to where he came from. I've missed him over the years, but there is something going on we don't know about and I'll be damned if I'll let you get hurt."

"Just don't kill each other. I've been trying to work everything out in my mind, and I keep coming back to your dad. Do you think he could have killed all those women?"

Luke parked the truck next to the house, killed the engine, and turned toward her. "I hate to say it, but I do."

The mood inside the house was anything but romantic. As much as he wanted to pull her into his arms and claim her lips, it wasn't happening. It wasn't good timing. Meg stood looking out the window, shifting her weight from one leg to the other.

"He doesn't have far to walk. I wouldn't worry about him."

Meg turned and frowned. "I know I'm just trying to figure out why he's been acting like such a jerk. He used to be a nice guy. Did you really think he was dead? How awful for you."

He shrugged. "My wanting you has nothing to do with the ranch. You know that, don't you?"

"Of course I do." She gave him a sincere smile. "Don't worry about his little remarks. I'm ignoring them and you should do the same. He's trying to bait you for some reason."

Luke walked to the window and put his arms around her waist. "I don't know what I've done right to deserve you. I appreciate your faith in me."

Her eyes shimmered when she gazed up at him. "Of course I have faith in you."

"I think I need to visit my father again tomorrow. He knows more than he's saying. I don't think a thing happened on the ranch without his knowledge. Plus, with his temper who would have dared?"

"Do you want me to go with you?"

He kissed the top of her head and pulled her closer to his side. "I need to do this alone."

Nodding, she stared out the window. "I can understand that. Have you decided which of the mustangs you plan to sell?"

"I had a list going before your dad died. A lot has happened in such a short time."

"It must be hard on you, too. I mean you lost your wife and daughter."

Luke nodded. "It's been hell except for the moments I share with you. I love you."

"I know. I love you too, and we'll get through this. I feel stronger with you by my side."

"Same here, sugar."

"I think we should look into what David has been doing the last few years. There must be an explanation for his behavior." She laid her head against his chest. "Something must have happened."

"I agree. Let's go upstairs." He leaned down and kissed her plump lips.

She moaned then pulled away. "David will be home soon. We'll have to wait until tonight."

"Tonight sounds good to me. I can't wait to make you scream again." He grinned at her watching her blush.

"I guess we'll have to tone it down a bit."

Luke laughed. "Not on your life. I don't do toned down with you. I have a need to give you all of me."

"I did enjoy all of you." She reached out and touched his chest. "It was wonderful, Luke. I really thought it wasn't for me. But you changed my mind."

"Good, I'm proud I made it good for you. We have something good together. Let's be sure no one tries to ruin it for us." He held his breath until she nodded.

David arrived home an hour later. Meg expected harsh words, but he hung his head and apologized. She hugged him.

"I think I should find somewhere else to stay." The pain reflected in his eyes tugged at her heart.

"No, David, we're family. We'll work it out."

Luke's eyes widened and he shook his head. "I'm not sure it's going to be so easy."

David sat on the couch and sighed. "I had time to think on my walk." He gave Luke a pointed look. "We might be able to talk it out and figure out what they hell happened on our land. We might have seen something and didn't realize it was important at the time."

She glanced at Luke as she sat down. "Sounds like a good idea."

"Luke?" David's voice was gruff.

"Sure why not?" He sat next to Meg. "Where should we start?"

"I don't remember any strangers around. Luke, do you remember any?"

"David, I've been asking myself the same thing. I don't remember anyone."

"What about Dad?"

Meg held her breath while she waited for Luke to answer.

"I just don't know. I have my suspicions, but I really don't know. He's a mean son of a bitch but I don't remember him being away from the ranch much. Where'd he find the girls?"

David pulled at his collar. "Well, it was worth a try to see if we knew anything. I am sorry for being such an ass." He smiled at Meg. "I will stay, thank you for asking me."

As she pushed to her feet, she caught Luke's intense stare at Davis and recoiled in surprise. They were still suspicious. Her theory was based on Harry doing it all, but there didn't seem to be proof. Actually, she didn't know what proof the police had. "Luke, could you work with Greg and make sure the ranch work is going well? I have a pile of paper work I need to weed through."

David stood. "I'll go with Luke and see what's what."

Luke glanced at her over David's head and frowned. "Let's go." He let David go ahead of him and before he walked out the door, he stared back at her and mouthed, "Thanks a lot."

This whole thing was taking up too much of their time. She should just let the police do their job. She had cattle to get to market and horses to sell. No more negativity, not while she was falling in love. Oh my, that man made her body sing. Who would have thought? Bedtime couldn't come fast enough for her.

Chapter Six

The desk appeared daunting, piled high with papers and unopened mail. A wave of panic set in at the sheer amount of responsibility on her shoulders. She rounded the desk and sat in her father's chair, tears filling her eyes. "I miss you, Dad." A heart-wrenching sob escaped her and she allowed herself to cry it out for a bit. The agony of her father being David's father, the despair of his death and the overwhelming fear of what was next poured down her face.

Things used to be so simple. Sure, she'd pined away for Luke for five long years, but the pain in her heart then was no comparison to what she felt now. All she wanted was to be able to relax again. Half the time she expected the police to show up and haul Luke away. Why had her father gone ahead and allowed digging on that particular part of the ranch?

The more she thought about it, the more it didn't make sense. He wouldn't have wanted condominiums so close to any land he owned. It was ridiculous really. Grabbing a clean bandana out of her jeans pocket, she dried her face. Crying time was over. She needed to keep the ranch going and profitable. Too many people relied on her for their livelihood. With a new determination, she started to tackle the piles of paper.

After a few long hours, she had everything put into the computer and it looked good. The numbers spoke for themselves; she had much more money than she'd ever thought. She'd ask Luke to look to be sure she was right. While she never wanted for anything, her dad made it seem as though they needed to watch their pennies.

Perhaps he was just being cautious for a rainy day, one of the years where everything went wrong and ranches went under. Sounded like something her dad would do. Scanning the cleared off desk, she sighed. Her sense of accomplishment had a layer of sadness under it. One day she hoped to remember her dad with sweet loving memories instead of despair. A part of her felt angry he had died, and as crazy as that was, she couldn't help it.

What could she do to help get this whole serial killer thing solved? Her blossoming romance with Luke hung under its shadow and she wanted her love to be full of sunshine. Laughing to herself, she pushed back from the desk and stood. Why not add flowers and goodness to her list? She guessed she was a romantic after all.

It was strange to imagine she'd want all the frills of new love. She'd spent years hardening her heart and her body, making herself into a no-nonsense ranch foreman. She hadn't allowed smiles or long looks into her life. Any man who tried to get close had been kicked to the curb. Luke had changed her, inside and out. She smiled; her heart was his.

Mounted on his horse, Luke took off his hat and wiped his brow with his shirtsleeve. He panned the terrain and frowned. "Where do you think those cattle went?"

David shrugged. "Are the fences between our place and Meg's still up, or did Owen take them down?"

Luke placed his hat back on his head, leaned both hands on the pommel and stretched his back. "They're down but for some reason the cattle don't migrate much over the border."

"We might as well ride. They must be somewhere." David kicked the sides of his roan and was off.

Luke watched him for a while before he followed. Something was still off with his brother. He was keeping something to himself and from Meg and it didn't sit well.

They rode across the two biggest pastures and then headed for the canyons. It was getting late, and he didn't want to be caught out in the dark. With his luck, it would be a cloudy, moonless night.

As they turned the corner into the opening of the nearest canyon, they heard a few of the cows bellowing. Glancing at each other, they rode on until they reached the herd.

"Dang, Luke, they act like they're lost. Did Meg turn them into pets or something?"

He shrugged and looked over the herd until he saw Old Sam the lead cow bull on the ground. "Guess Old Sam didn't teach the cattle to do anything but follow him. Strangest thing I've ever seen." He swung down and slowly approached the steer. "Damn he's been shot. He grabbed his rifle and carefully looked around.

David grabbed his rifle too. "I don't see anyone. Whoever it was is gone.

"The cattle probably scattered shortly after the shot and are just now getting back together. I'd better call Meg." He got back on his horse and it wasn't until he rode out of the canyon that he found phone reception. He talked to Meg and rode back.

"Did you call the police?"

Luke shook his head. "No, I only called Meg. I'm done with those yahoos. They couldn't find their asses if they were handed to them. They still think I killed all those girls."

"It's going to be dark soon. Are you up for spending the night?" David grinned.

"I sure am. We used to camp out a lot. Those were some good times."

David's grin faded. "Yes, they were. Haven't had times like that since I left. I have to say I was surprised you left. I pictured you and Meg together with a couple kids by now. Strange how things don't turn out the way you think."

Luke raised his eyebrows and opened his mouth.

"Save it we'd better gather some wood for a fire. We have all night to yap." David walked toward the treed hillside.

They'd be yapping, and he was going to figure out what was going on. David's constant change in mood bothered him. Serial killers were moody, weren't they? Maybe they were crazy, not moody. As far as he knew, they hadn't identified any of the bodies yet. Sighing, he started for the trees. How he wished he were with Meg right now, making love to her.

David dragged an old log over and sat in front of the fire. The orange glow from the flames danced across his face in sinister ways. Was it the flickering that gave him a look of evil? Or something else? No, it had to be his imagination. Still, Luke's body remained tense, and he couldn't get it to relax.

"So, what's for dinner?" David cocked his left eyebrow at Luke.

"Granola bars and water." He tried hard to stop his lips from twitching.

"You're kidding right? Don't you carry more with you?" David sounded annoyed.

"What do you have to contribute to our feast?"

David grumbled. "I'll take a granola bar. I've seen them on the shelves in the grocery store, but I never realized people actually eat them."

"These are much better than they used to be." He reached into his saddlebag, grabbed a bar and tossed it to David. He reached in again to get one for himself. He heard the rustling of the wrapper being opened and when he glanced up, David had already devoured it.

"Not bad. Got any more?"

"I have a box of them." He put the box on the ground between them. "Help yourself."

"I've scanned the canyon up and down, and I haven't seen anyone around. It's odd the steer was shot. Maybe it's connected to the murders."

Luke pushed his hat back on his head. "Why do you think that?"

David shrugged. "Maybe someone wants the land and figured they can get it pretty cheap since part of it is a crime scene and all."

"Makes as much sense as anything else. I don't know what to think anymore." He paused and stared into the flames. "David, why did you leave?"

"Dad and I weren't getting along."

"I don't want the bull answer. I want the truth."

David stared at him for a while. "I brought home a girl that night, and when I went inside to grab a few beers…" He took a deep breath. "When I came back, Dad was all over her, and she wasn't willing. I tried to stop him, but he beat me to a pulp in his rage, and I could hear him go after the girl again. I came to and she was gone. Dad said he drove her home. We had words and he told me to leave and never come back." Wiping his hand over his face, David shook his head. "He said he paid her enough money to keep her mouth shut, but if push came to shove, she'd identify me as the attacker."

"What girl?"

"I picked her up at Cappy's Bar over in the next town. I'm not even sure what her name was. I took off, he had me so afraid of going to jail. I kept track of the news but I never saw anything about it."

"Oh, God, I'm so sorry, David. What a mean son of a bitch!" He wanted to confess his role of burying the girl's body but he didn't dare. How could he have not known the body was a female? It was heavy as hell but at the time, his mind was going in circles and he was full of terror. "We'll have to go to the police about it."

Sighing, David nodded.

Suddenly a shot rang out, it's explosive report echoing through the canyon.

Dust kicked up as the next shot hit the dirt near Luke's feet. He yelled for David, and they both scrambled for cover, throwing themselves behind some boulders. "What the hell is going on?"

"Looks to me like someone is aiming to kill us." David nodded at the Winchester clutched in Luke's hands.

"Glad we both thought quick and grabbed our rifles before dodging for cover."

"Did you see where the shots came from?"

David shook his head. "Not exactly. Near as I can tell it was from the west wall."

"Son of a bitch. Cattle rustlers?"

David shrugged. "I doubt it. I think someone is trying to keep us off Dad's property."

Another shot rang out, and they both instinctively ducked as pieces of rock showered them. Their eyes were wide as they gazed at each other.

"We need to move. Isn't there a cave in this canyon?" David asked.

Luke sighed. "Yes and it's on the west wall. Must be where the shooter is holed up."

"He's got the vantage point. Luke, we need to get out of here."

"Cover me, I'll grab the horses."

David laughed. "Like you can run fast. You were lucky enough to get to safety with that bum leg of yours."

Luke swallowed his pride. "I'll cover you, just be quick, and stay low."

"That was my plan." David ran and the shooting started.

Luke got off shot after shot and kept the cave dweller at bay. It was only a minute but it seemed so much longer as Luke waited, holding his breath, for David.

David raced back and threw the reins to Luke's horse to him. "Get out of here! I'll cover you. We don't have time to argue."

Luke nodded. He wanted to say something to David just in case, but there wasn't time. He took the reins, grabbed the horse's mane, pulled himself up, and rode. It didn't feel right leaving David there alone. If anything happened…

More shots echoed through the night, and he waited at the mouth of the canyon, rifle in hand. Then there was silence. His heart sank as the silence grew. He was going to kill that son of a bitch. He dug his heels into the horse's sides and started to race into the canyon as though the flames of hell were behind him. He readied his rifle and aimed at the cave. Out of the corner of his eye, he saw David racing toward him on his horse.

"I must have got him. We'd better get to where we can call out. The police will have to be the ones to figure this all out. It's too dark for us to go looking."

Luke took slow breaths as he turned his horse around and rode beside David out of the canyon. They'd come back for the cattle. Finally, his heart stopped pounding so hard. If anything had happened to David, he would never have forgiven himself. Maybe it was time to tell what he knew. It wasn't worth his brother's life to keep from going to jail.

They slowed their mounts and then came to a stop. Luke took out his phone and dialed 911.

The terrain was too rugged for the police to get to the canyon that night. They'd see about getting a helicopter there in the morning.

Luke and David slowly made their way to the house. Luke wasn't taking any chances with the horses. One misstep and they could be hurt, yet they needed to be as far away from the canyon as possible. The shooter might not have acted alone. His heart pounded. Meg could be in danger.

It had been one thing after another since he came back. What were the odds? Maybe he was just bad luck. He wanted to be able to run into the house, grab up Meg, and take her to bed, but it wouldn't be fair to her anymore. Trouble followed him and he didn't want anything to happen to her.

The loss of his loving future pierced his heart. What if he couldn't go on without her? She wasn't bound to agree to the break up, but it was for the best. Damn, and he didn't have near enough time with her. A lifetime wouldn't have been enough.

"Luke? Earth to, Luke."

Glancing to his right he cocked his eyebrow. "What?"

"Look." David pointed into the night. "The lights are on at the house. You can just begin to see them."

His stomach dropped. "I hope she's okay."

"I'm sure she is."

"I wish we could ride faster. I feel so helpless."

"We'll get there." David reassured him.

They rode, and as the house came into sight, they could see a police car. Luke called the police station and they informed him Meg was fine. The police were waiting for the two brothers to return home. A sigh of relief escaped him.

Finally, he was close enough to see Meg and his eyes feasted on the sight of her. How was he going to let her go? Love for her ingrained his whole body and he prayed for strength. After all, it was for her own good.

Her face lit up as their gazes locked, and her smile was pull of hope. She hurried toward him and when he hit the ground, she flew into his arms. He dropped the reins and held her to him savoring the feel of her against him. He'd already lost so much; how could he walk away from his true love?

"I'm so glad you're safe," she whispered against his ear.

"I'm just glad nothing went on here. I don't know who was in the canyon." Stepping back, he cupped her cheeks and stared at her lovely lips. If only...

"Luke, the police need a statement," David called from the front steps.

He dropped his hands, gave her one last look, and walked away. Coldness shrouded him and encased his heart. No one had ever said life was fair. The only honorable thing left was to protect the ones he loved.

Luke nodded at Detective Timbers. "I need to speak with you." He could see the questions in Meg's eyes. "It's fine. I'll be right back." Leaving her side chilled him. He walked toward Timbers and both men went into the house.

"What is it?" Timbers eagerness disgusted Luke.

"I think we should talk in the office." He led the way, wondering the whole time if he was doing the right thing. Protecting Meg and David was his main concern. He didn't know why they had been shot at, but maybe the truth would make it stop.

"Have a seat." He gestured toward a chair in front of the big desk. It felt a bit odd sitting behind the desk and having Timbers on the other side. From the frown on Timber's face, he didn't like the set up.

"You have something to tell me?" Timbers leaned forward.

"I believe my father killed those women." His throat felt sandpaper dry.

"Your father? I had considered it at one time, but I don't think—"

"This isn't about what you think. It's about what I know." Luke jumped up and began to pace behind the desk. "I helped my dad bury one of the bodies."

Timbers stood up clutching his gun in his hand. "Sit down slowly and keep your hands on the desk."

Shaking his head, he did as Timbers asked. "I didn't know it was one of the women at the time."

"What the hell did you think you were burying? A dead dog?" His voice rose with each question.

"No, I thought I was burying my brother." The room grew silent as they stared at each other.

"So, you bury your brother and you thought it was okay? What the hell is wrong with the whole Kelly family? In what world is it fine to help bury your brother? You'd better start at the beginning."

Luke swallowed hard and ran his fingers through his hair.

"Hands on the desk."

He placed his hands on the desk. "The night David left, I thought I had buried him. I didn't know he'd run off. My father told me it was an accident, and we had to bury him or we'd both go to jail. I helped to put the body in the truck bed, and I even dug the hole. I left that same night and stayed away for five years." He sat back in the chair, exhausted.

"So, let's pretend I believe you. Why didn't you say something as soon as the first body was found? This does not look good. I believe you and David did this together."

"David had nothing to do with it. Dad knocked him out and stole his girl. That is whose body you found, the first one. I don't know who was shooting at us tonight. I don't know if it was connected or not."

Timbers' eyes widened as his lips formed a tight, straight line. "Stand up and put your hands behind your head. I'm taking you in. I don't know who you think you are fooling with your bizarre story, but it doesn't add up."

Luke stood and did as directed. He closed his eyes as the hand cuffs went on. "This is why I didn't speak up before. I knew you'd throw me in jail." His words were laced with the same bitterness he held in his heart.

Fear clutched her heart as she watched Luke ride away in the police car. What had he said to Timbers to be arrested? David didn't seem surprised. He shrugged his shoulders and went inside the house as though he hadn't a care in the world. Did he already know what Luke had told Timbers?

Her head swirled with worry, and her heart hadn't stopped pounding since she had heard about the shots fired. Luke was safe, but it didn't stop the intense fear. Standing outside in the dark, she saw David inside talking to the police. There was only one way to find out what he was saying. She headed inside.

"If he said he buried a body, he must be involved," David said in a loud, calm voice. "I just wish I had known. I could have saved a few lives."

"So you had no reason to suspect him? He hadn't acted strange at all?" Meg walked into the room and stared at David waiting for him to answer the officer's question.

"Not at the time. Tonight, though, he did say he had to confess to Meg." He glanced in her direction and gave her a sympathetic smile. "I'm sorry, Meg. I can't believe it myself, and he's my brother."

She clasped her hands together to stop them from shaking. Her stomach dropped and she felt a bit faint. "Luke confessed to something? Confessed to what?"

David stood and put his hand on the small of her back. "Come, sit down. You look white as a ghost."

"I do feel a bit shaky." She sat on the couch, and David sat next to her. Immediately she moved over to put more space between them. Something was wrong, and she didn't trust him.

David sighed noisily. "I wish I had good news for you, Meg, but it looks as though Luke is the killer. He told me he buried the first body. Why he didn't confess to more, I have no idea except for maybe he wants to use the rest of his confession as leverage against the death penalty."

She gasped and covered her mouth with her hand. Her eyes widened as she looked at one police officer to the other, then finally at David. They all believed him. Dropping her hand back into her lap, she shook her head. "I don't know what is going on here but you're lying. Luke would never kill anyone!"

"Whoa now, he never mentioned killing just burying. But you have to admit it isn't a far stretch from burying to killing." David slowly shook his head. "I have a feeling the shooting tonight is tied to Luke. Someone else must know or maybe Luke hired someone to take pot shots at us."

"Why on earth would he do that?"

"He wants your land. I think he has some grand plan to scare you away from the ranch. I thought he'd marry you to get the land, but now I'm thinking he doesn't want to go to the bother."

"The bother? You know, the more you talk, the less I believe you. Luke loves me."

His eyebrows rose. "Is that what he told you?"

Her stomach clenched. "Yes, he told me he loves me, and I believe him."

David smirked. "Did he show you a good time in bed?"

Rage filled her as she stood up and slapped David across the face. "I don't know why you think you have the right to speak to me in such a way. Whether Luke loves me or not is between us. It has nothing to do with you." Her voice shook and sounded high-pitched. Quickly she took a step back, waiting for David to retaliate.

He rubbed the red mark on his cheek slowly, studying her the whole time. "You're right and I'm sorry. You know, even though Harry beat the hell out of both of us, I could see the approval in his eyes for Luke. Never for me. Never a smile or word of praise for me, ever. I wished I could run away and come live here with your family. Stupid really."

Shaking her head, she sat next to him. "I'm sorry I hit you. Harry is a monster all around. He knows much more than he's saying, and good or bad we need the truth."

David stared at nothing in particular. Probably trying to gather his thoughts. She didn't say another word.

Finally, he shrugged. "I guess you're right. Luke says he's still sharp as a tack and the police think he's off his rocker. I just can't bring myself to see the old man again. Would you go with me?"

"Of course, but first I need to call Luke's Lawyer, and I'm going down to the police station."

"I doubt there is much you can do tonight."

Standing she straightened her shoulders. "You might be right but I need to be there. He'd do the same for me, and I love him. I know he's innocent. He's no killer."

"He might not be a killer but he buried a body. That's serious."

She nodded as she grabbed her cellphone and sweater. She was out the door before he had a chance to invite himself along. She needed time alone without David planting doubts in her mind. He was right about one thing; Harry needed to come clean and soon.

Her heart beat painfully against her chest as she thought about Luke in jail or worse, being interrogated by Timbers. If he weren't the sheriff's cousin, he probably wouldn't be given such latitude to arrest people whenever he felt like it.

The truck slid as she slammed on the brakes to turn into the police station parking lot. She hadn't realized she'd been driving so fast. Taking a deep breath, she tried to calm herself as she parked. She turned off the engine and closed her eyes, saying a quick prayer for Luke. She needed to pull herself together. He needed her and he needed her to be strong.

He loved her didn't he? She flew out the truck, slammed the door, and hurried across the parking lot to the front door. Of course, he loved her. Damn David for putting doubts into her head.

The aging desk Sargent scowled at her as she came through the door. "You might as well go home. They won't let you see him."

Her heart dropped. "Is his lawyer here?"

"Sure is, but I'm not sure there's a thing he could say to save Luke. I'd say his fate is sealed. Go on home."

His fate is sealed? It just couldn't be true. Why was everyone so quick to believe him guilty? She glanced at her watch. It was only one in the morning. Yanking the door open, she shot out of the station, scrambled to her truck and hopped in. Going home to David was not an appetizing option. She drove out of the parking lot and down the main street to Benny's Diner. It was open twenty-four hours a day. Coffee sounded good, and hopefully, she'd have a chance to think.

She pulled her wool sweater tighter around her as she ran from the truck to the diner. It was cold out. She opted for a booth in the corner where she could look out the front window. She nodded at the pretty waitress as she started to pour her coffee.

"What else can I get you?"

"Evie, I just don't know. How about some toast to start with?"

"You got it, sugar."

Her hands warmed instantly as she wrapped them around her mug. Life had been peaceful before Luke came back. She'd always felt a constant ache while he was gone, but she'd been as much at peace as she could possibly be. Now her father was dead, Luke was in jail, and David... well, she still wasn't sure about David.

The bell over the diner door jingled as the door opened and Benny ambled in. "Colder than a witch's... Hi ya, Meg, good to see you."

He shed his coat and put it the counter. Evie, quickly grabbed it and carried it into the back. Benny sat down across from Meg. "I've never known you to be a late-night coffee drinker."

Benny had been one of her father's best friends. "Usually I'm not, Benny." The concern in his dark brown eyes was her undoing and tears started to fall.

"Meg, tell me what's got you turning on the waterworks."

She stared at the gray-haired man and nodded. "It's a long story."

"I have time."

She poured her heart out to Benny, who nodded a few times. It felt good to talk to someone.

"Well, first of all, Harry never owned that land. It had always belonged to your father. He leased it to Harry until David came along. Then Harry threatened to ruin your dad and never paid a penny after that. In fact, your dad loaned him money a time or two when it looked as though they were going under. The money was never repaid. Harry also took great delight telling your dad how he treated David." Benny paused when Evie approached the table with toast and coffee. "Morning, Evie."

Evie blushed and said a soft good morning back. Benny watched her the whole way back to the counter.

"Where was I? Oh, Harry was always bragging he was going to ruin Owen and his family. He'd get his and stuff like that. He was a big drinker, and most folks didn't take him seriously. He got back at his wife plenty. He was always running around on her. What those pretty young things saw in him, I'll never know. A few I think he paid."

"Wow. But Harry sold the house."

"He did. It was all he owned with the provision he allowed his wife to stay as long as she wanted. The provision wasn't enforceable, but Harry didn't know that."

"There have been so many secrets since my dad's death. I swear my head is spinning."

"I don't blame you there. That Luke of yours is a good man. Now David, there has always been something not quite right about him. I could never put my finger on it. And Harry is as crazy as they come."

She nodded. "There's crazy and then there is really crazy. There's nothing wrong with Harry but half the town believes he has Alzheimer's."

"I heard that rumor too. I hope they let Luke go soon."

"You already know he's in jail?"

He smiled. "Not much gets by me. I have folks telling me stuff all day long as though I was some type of priest. It's amazing how much people talk. Are the authorities going to talk to Harry? I think he's behind this whole fiasco. Your cattle problems too."

"Thanks, Benny. I appreciate the info."

Benny stood up and winked. "You need anything let me know."

She watched him go into the kitchen. She'd always thought Harry had something to do with the whole thing. It was hard to believe her dad had owned all the land this whole time and had still wanted David and Luke to have a share. Her dad was a good man. You couldn't judge someone from one mistake. Even if it was a huge mistake. Could it be Harry? He wouldn't have had a way to shoot at Luke and David. Had her dad known about the cabin?

"More coffee?" Evie asked. The coffee pot hovered over the mug.

"I'd better head on home. I need to get to the canyon as soon as the sun rises."

"You only have about an hour now."

Meg's eyes widened. "I've been sitting here that long?"

"You sure have. I hope you found answers to what's troubling you. You have a good day now."

Meg sat there another minute before she took money out of her purse and left it on the table. Luke had his lawyer, and she needed to check on the cattle. David would probably want to go with her. "Thanks, Evie!" she called as she headed out the door.

She'd have just enough time to change her clothes before sunup. Whoever had killed her bull was in big trouble. That damn bull had cost a ton but he threw good calves. He hadn't been with the rest of the cattle so how they all ended up in the canyon together was a mystery.

The light was on in the house, and she sighed. That meant David was probably up, and she wasn't in the mood to talk to him. Her best bet was to ignore him if possible. She wouldn't take his bait and have him give her more reasons why it had to be Luke behind all of the trouble.

Meg got out of the truck and walked into the house. David lounged against the counter right next to the coffee pot. She thought she saw a glint of humor in his eyes, but it disappeared so quickly she could have imagined it.

"I was getting worried about you. I called the station and they told me you'd left hours ago."

"Luke's lawyer was there, and they weren't going to allow me to see him."

"Where were you?" His eyes narrowed as he stared at her.

"At Benny's. Benny and my dad were good friends." She waited for his reaction. She didn't trust him.

"Yes they were." He set his mug on the counter. I'll saddle up the horses. It'll be daylight soon."

She nodded. "I'll need a minute to change clothes. I'll meet you at the barn."

He stared at her again. "Okay. See you in a few."

When he finally left, she headed toward her room. It wasn't until she opened one of her dresser drawers that she noticed things were out of place. She opened the rest of her drawers and things had been shuffled around as if someone was looking for something. It had to be David, but what was he looking for? Now she doubly dreaded riding out with him. After she changed, she grabbed her handgun out of the lockbox and put it in her saddlebag. Better safe than sorry where he was concerned.

Her nerves started to fray. How could this be happening? Maybe she should just wait for Wayne and his deputies to show up, but that could take hours. Grabbing the saddlebag, she headed to the barn.

"Ready?" David asked. He looked as tired as she felt. At least she'd combed her hair and didn't look scruffy.

She secured her bag and got on Merry's back. "Let's go." She turned the horse and off they went. She tried to stay just far enough ahead of David to avoid talking to him. He kept catching up. So she tried to keep behind him, but he slowed. Plastering a fake smile on her face, she hoped she was hiding her annoyance.

"We should be there soon."

She nodded. "Just around the bend." She heard the helicopter before she saw it and sighed. "Let's pick up the pace. I don't want to miss anything."

They got there just after the chopper put down. Wayne had two of his deputies with him. As soon as all the noise stopped, she jumped down, gave Merry a soothing pat on her muzzle, and joined the sheriff.

"Don't get too close," He warned. "The feds will be here soon."

"What—?"

David came to her side. "What does the FBI have to do with a dead bull? You'd think they'd want to handle the case against Luke."

The clenching of her stomach was only the beginning of her pain. Her heart squeezed and her head ached. *Case against Luke?* David knew more than he was saying. He didn't seem to be too upset about Luke being in jail accused of being a serial killer. To keep from flying apart, she folded her arms in front of her.

Chapter Seven

"There seems to be some evidence the killings and the events of last night are connected. The FBI has been working on the case off site." Wayne smiled at her. "Don't you worry we'll get the right person behind bars."

She recognized the look; Wayne knew Luke was innocent. She wanted to weep with relief. There was too much pent up emotion inside her trying to burst out. Another helicopter flew into the canyon, and she set her focus on it. Two men got out. Both were tall and blond. One wore dress shoes and the other boots. It made her smile. The one wearing the boots was the trustworthy one as far as she was concerned.

The new comers didn't acknowledge anyone at first. Instead, they walked over to the dead bull and began to scan the walls of the canyon. The one wearing the boots pointed to the cave and began to walk toward it. The other man shook his head and followed. His feet were bound to hurt after a bit, the walls looked closer than they actually were.

"How'd they know about the cave?" David asked.

"From the statements you and Luke gave last night." The sheriff's brow furrowed. "Why? Was there another way they might have known?"

"No, no. Just making an observation."

"I have cattle missing, a dead bull, and most important, Luke is in jail. Wayne, do you have any ideas for a game plan?"

David's mouth opened; then he closed it. He jutted out his bottom lip as though he was pouting. Why hadn't she ever noticed that expression before?

"Darlin', I'd tell you to go home and let me worry about it but I know you. You won't go home. Tell you what. The Millers called. It appears a few of your cattle found their garden. I bet the others are scattered."

"Yes, Greg is having the men search for them."

"Good. Are you up to a ride in a helicopter?"

"I don't know—"

Wayne gave David a sour glance. "I didn't ask you."

Meg nodded. "Sure. Where to?"

"The station. I think you'll be interested in what we found out. By the way, David, I need you to put your hands behind your back. Deputy Ford here will take care of you. And Meg, Deputy Green will get your horses back to your place."

Before she had a chance to see David cuffed, Wayne whisked her away toward the copter. She tried to ask a few questions, but he motioned he couldn't hear her. Looking down she saw David put into the other helicopter. He was her brother, but she didn't feel a connection to him, and if he had anything to do with Luke being behind bars, heaven help him.

Once they all arrived at the station, Meg began to ask questions, but Wayne put her off. He led her to the interrogation room. Dread filled her as he opened the door. Luke sat in a chair looking anything but happy. His eyes lit up when he saw her.

"Are you all right? They wouldn't allow me to see you."

"I'm fine. No matter what happens, I need you to know I love you so much. You've become everything to me." His stare was intense.

"I know, I love you too."

The door opened, and David nearly stumbled as he was shoved inside, still handcuffed. They unlocked one of the cuffs and locked it to the table. Before they could say a word, Harry was brought in and shown to a chair.

"What is this? Some damned family reunion? You have no right to bring me here," Harry snarled.

The FBI agent with the boots walked in. "I'm Special Agent Jeffries, and I have a slew of questions for y'all."

Everyone exchanged glances, but all Meg saw was worry.

"How about we start with the lies?" Jeffries paced back and forth in front of the mirror. "Lie number one: David is not Owen O'Brien's son, he is Harry's. Why Harry perpetrated the lie is something I intend to find out."

Meg gasped and gave Harry a hard look. "But—"

Jeffries put his hand up. "No questions yet. Lie number two: Owen owned the land you claimed to be yours. My theory is you found about the affair and intended to have Owen pay so you blackmailed him by saying David was his son. Why not have him deed you the land?"

Harry's face grew red with fury but he remained silent.

Meg reached over and grabbed Luke's hand. The returning squeeze gave her the strength to go on.

"Lie number three: Harry, you told Luke he was helping you to bury his brother. Luke it must have been a heavy burden to carry all these years, though I would have loved to have seen your expression when you saw David alive. The main thing is you came clean about it."

Meg snatched her hand back as her stomach dropped.

"David, you claim you left because of a fight, but you forgot to mention how your father raped your girl. You knew when the first body surfaced who it was, yet you never said a word. In fact, you seemed content to have your brother go to jail." Jeffries stopped pacing and stared each of them down. "I'd go on, but there are too many lies to count."

The agent held a hand up as though to forestall any arguments. "Now, I don't usually do a group interrogation, but with all the untruths interconnected, I thought it best. First of all, the shooting in the canyon and the murders are not connected. Yeah, David, I found the shooter and he's a big talker. According to him, you wanted all the land for yourself. He mentioned something about a plan to get rid of Luke first." He shook his head and settled his gaze on Luke. "Nasty business, that is. He needed to get to you before Meg signed over the land. He was afraid you'd get married, and he'd miss his chance to claim his supposed birthright."

"That's a lie!" David tried to stand but the handcuffs prevented it.

"Of course there is the little matter of all the dead women. Meg you might be interested to know your father's fingerprints were on the camera discovered up there. An old sweater of his was found near the cabin. Luke also told us about the cabin."

Meg felt the blood drain from her face. *My father?*

"It threw us for a minute, but I didn't buy it. We also received a handwritten letter accusing Owen of the murders." Jeffries paused and stared pointedly at Harry. "Nice try."

"Now see here," Harry sputtered, his face turning dark.

"Normally, I don't show my hand, but I think between all of you we might just get the full story. So, that led us to wonder who hated your father so much they'd want to frame him. David here is a real good choice for a suspect. He omitted a lot but I don't think he has the stomach for killing, at least not doing it himself. No, David is more the type who pays people to get rid of those in his way. Now Harry here, really is a mean son of a gun."

"This all about revenge and land?" Meg's voice was shaky. She glanced from David to Harry in disgust. "I can't be in the same room as them." She stood and rushed out the door. She didn't stop until she was outside. Leaning against the brick building, she took a deep breath as her eyes began to fill. Monsters! She'd been surrounded by monsters. Yes, her dad had made a mistake, but he'd paid a hefty price through the years, with the suffering he'd endured thinking his son was being abused. Her shoulders slumped. He should have called the authorities. David and Luke hadn't deserved the abuse they got. All the men in her life had lied to her. Her heart squeezed, and her stomach threatened to heave.

Luke had lied and her dad had lied. Luke thought he'd buried David and had never told anyone? How was that possible? Who did something like that? Why would *he* do that?

Swiping at her tears with the back of her hand, she pushed away from the wall. She had a ranch to run, cattle to round up, and horses to sell. She'd done it all before and she'd do it again. She'd faced down heartache before and by God, she'd do it again.

Deputy Ford walked out the door and stopped in front of her. "Need a ride home?"

"I'm allowed to leave?"

"You're the only one not involved. I'll drive you."

His gentle nature had a calming effect, and she nodded. "I'd like to go home."

He opened the car door and closed it for her after she got in. She always thought she'd be fascinated riding in a police car but not today. She stared out the window, barely seeing the world as they passed it by. Her thoughts were of her father and the decisions he'd made. She'd hardly had time to mourn him and now this. Swallowing hard, she clasped her shaking hands together. A few more miles and she'd be able to cry out her heartbreak.

Deputy Ford parked, got out of the car and opened her door for her. He seemed to know she didn't want to talk. He tipped his hat to her after she got out, and then he was off.

She stood in her yard as a slight breeze lifted her hair and blew it around her shoulders. The birds chirped, all welcoming her back at the same time. She wished it would bring her some solace but it didn't. Quickly she went to the barn and poked her head in. The men were still out rounding up the cattle. She'd call Greg in a bit, after she got herself together.

She'd been the biggest of fools, trusting every word said. Her whole life was a lie but she had allowed it to happen. She should have asked more questions, she should have... Hell, she didn't even know what would have helped. It had never occurred to her the people in her life would lie to her. Perhaps she was too gullible or maybe just plain stupid.

Shaking her head, she went into the house and sat on the couch. She'd lived next to a serial killer all her life. The man she loved had buried a murder victim. Her body began to shake, and she couldn't seem to control it. She had allowed David to live in her house when he planned to kill both her and Luke. Tears rolled down her face so fast she didn't try to stem the flow. It was all too much to bear, and sobs racked her body. And Luke... Pretending a brother he thought he buried was alive? No wonder he'd seemed skeptical when she told him David had returned. And yet he still had said nothing.

Her broken heart of the last five years was nothing compared to the pain she now felt.

She cried until there were no more tears left. Her heart and soul were broken beyond repair, and she felt purposeless. Grabbing a few tissues, she mopped up her tears. Then she fished her cellphone out of her pocket and called Greg, hoping her voice wouldn't give out.

It was good news; they'd located most of the cattle. The death of the bull was a big loss, but compared to everything else it wasn't so big. Greg had the men fixing the cut fences and then they'd be in. She tried to sound happy and told him "good job" but her words sounded hollow to her.

Meg wandered into the office and her spirit died. Harry must have had more than an affair to blackmail her father with. Plopping down into the chair—his chair—she glanced around the room. Why hadn't he told her about the land? It was then she realized he'd been lied to as well. He'd thought David was his son, and who knew how many threats Harry had made? He must have threatened more than telling the truth. A shiver invaded her. Lord only knew what Harry had said.

She wished she could just up and leave the whole place behind. Yet it would be all she'd have to fill her. She'd done it when Luke left before, but there was so much emptiness inside her now. *Damn him!* He had her thinking about babies and a happily ever after. Now there wouldn't be any of it. She had a bull to replace, cattle to round up, and horses to sell. Maybe if she kept telling herself all the things she needed to do, she wouldn't feel so adrift.

She'd ask one of the men to pack up Luke and David's things. They had no claim to the land, and she wanted them erased from her life. If only she could erase them from her mind and heart. Tears threatened again, and she slammed her hand down on the desk. Somehow, she'd have to find the strength inside her and ride it out.

Luke just stared from his brother to his father. *What the hell?* This was his family and yet they were total strangers. David, his protector, wanted him dead, and his worthless father had killed those women? It all had to be some cruel joke. He should have never come back. His heart wrenched. Meg would never believe him again. The look on her face when Jeffries told her he thought he'd buried his own brother was one of horror and disbelief. It would forever be burned into Luke's mind.

"David, you were going to let me take the fall for the murders?"

David smiled. "It seemed as easy as killing you. Easier, I think. With you locked away, Meg would naturally turn to her brother to help with the ranch. We all know ranching is a dangerous business. Accidents happen all the time."

"You piece of filth!" He jumped up trying to get to David but the deputies were quick and sat him back down.

David glanced at Harry with hate in his eyes. "What about you? You knew I wasn't a bastard but kept calling me one?"

Harry gave them a triumphant smile. "I made money off my brilliant idea. No one touches what's mine. Came pretty close to killing the girl, but she'd never come anywhere near me. I even tried following her, but somehow she'd sense me and take her damn horse on trails I didn't know about."

Luke's body tensed. "You are lower than low, and the worst part is you aren't insane. You are plain evil, and may you rot in hell!"

Harry laughed. "You'll be right there with me boy or did you forget you helped bury that sweet thing your brother brought home?"

Jeffries had been quietly observing them. "Luke you're free to go. Don't leave the county. I'm going to need a few statements from you. You'll be at the O'Brien place?"

Stunned, he suddenly realized he didn't know where he'd be.

"He'll probably be at the motel down the road." Harry nodded. "She won't want him after today."

Luke had thought his heart hurt as much as it could until Harry opened his mouth. It was true Meg wouldn't forgive him. Why should she? He and his family brought her into this whole nightmare. "I'll go get my stuff and yes I'll probably be at the hotel. I won't leave the county."

Jeffries nodded. "Get out of here then."

He didn't need it repeated. He left in a flash, not looking back. *Damn he didn't have a ride home.*

"Did you need to use the phone?" Wayne asked him.

He hesitated so long; Wayne grabbed his Stetson and put it on his head. "Come on, I'll drive you out there.

The drive was silent. Luke had too much going on in his head to keep a conversation going. He almost told Wayne to turn around and drive him to the motel but he needed to face Meg no matter how much it was going to hurt.

He still felt the pain of losing his wife and daughter but he'd been healing. Now it was as though the scab had been ripped opened and bled once again. This time he didn't think a scab would get a chance to form. His jaw hurt from clenching it so tight. What was he going to say to Meg? He should have told her about the body he'd buried long ago. How many times had he lied to her about David?

The ranch house came into view, and his heart pounded painfully against his chest. He already knew it but he had to hear it from her. He'd lost everything. The car slowed and stopped. He thanked Wayne as he got out then stood in the yard, gathering his courage to face Meg. Why did everything have to be so hard? He loved her with everything in him, but it wasn't enough. He wasn't enough, and it was his own doing.

The contents on the porch caused his stomach to lurch. His meager belongings were out there waiting to be picked up. She obviously didn't want to see him. Maybe it was for the best. He didn't have enough energy to face her.

He saw a flutter from the curtain in the main room and he knew she was watching him.

It hurt to know she wasn't going to come out and say goodbye.

"Need a ride?" Greg asked as he ambled over.

Luke sighed. "Looks like I do."

"Let's get your stuff into the truck, and I'll take you to the motel unless you have somewhere else you'd like me to drop you."

"The motel is fine. Thanks, Greg."

As they loaded a small suitcase and a few small boxes into the back of the pickup, he could tell she was still standing at the window watching. He wished he had enough guts to go in and talk things out with Meg but he didn't dare.

Greg chatted the whole ride into town, and by the time they got to the motel, Luke had a major headache. He quickly unloaded his stuff onto the sidewalk in front of the motel office. "Greg, look after her for me."

Greg gave him a sad smile. "Don't you worry."

Luke nodded, walked into the office, and registered. He got the key and then gathered his belongings and went into room 107. It was clean but small and incredibly lonely. Maybe he should have stopped at the liquor store for a bottle of whiskey. Dropping his things just inside, he shook his head as he closed the door. Even whiskey would be bad company tonight.

The bed creaked as he sat on it. Tossing his hat across the room to the small table, he let out a loud groan of anguish. His insides felt twisted and his heart shredded. He could blame his father and his brother but it was his doing. Why hadn't he spoken up? Why hadn't he at least confided in Meg? His sweet loving Meg was his no longer.

A lone tear trailed down his face. It was worse than when they had told him his wife and daughter were dead. Now it was pain piled up on top of pain, and he didn't think he'd ever get out from under it all.

The next morning Meg woke to a house that was much too quiet. Her first thought was *Luke lied*. Drawing in the shaky breath, torment washed over her. She started to repeat to herself, "I have a ranch to run."

She pulled on her old jeans and black T-shirt, stopping only to quickly brush her teeth and hair before she headed into the kitchen. Making coffee was automatic to her and she pulled on her boots as it brewed. After pouring it into a travel mug, she grabbed her hat, gloves and jacket. Work should help, she hoped.

When she got to the barn, Greg was already there with Merry saddled. "I figured you'd want to head out early today. Want company?"

"No, Greg, but thank you. I have some thinking to do, and I want to check on the mustangs." She gave him a sad smile. "You probably did that yesterday, didn't you?"

"Yes, ma'am."

"Thanks, Greg." She kicked Merry's sides and off they went. As she rode, a bit of tension left her body. Her father must have had his reasons. What did her mother know? What did her say? She must have known about the land, and she'd never said a word. There had been times her parents would stop talking when she entered the room, but she had always assumed it was boring adult stuff.

She rode until she spotted the herd. Funny how she always thought of the land as the Kelly's and the horses Luke's. It had been her hope that Luke would be back, she supposed. She'd be more careful with her wishes in the future.

Her heart was like a big piece of lead in her chest. Was it only a few days ago they had made love? Oh, how he made her body and soul sing. Nothing would ever be the same again. She'd go back to her old life of concentrating on the ranch, alone. It was fine before and it would be fine again.

Shaking her head she gave a halfhearted laugh. Who was she kidding? The hole in her heart was way too big to fill even with the amount of work it took to run a ranch.

She wished she'd never known how good intimacy could be or that a love so deep existed. She straightened her shoulders. She was as tough as they came, and she needed to remember that. She pulled Merry to a halt and watched the mustangs play. They seemed frisky today, running after one another, rolling on the ground. She'd put off selling some of them. She didn't have it in her now.

"Come on, Merry, it's time to go home." She turned her horse and off they went. She stopped here and there to check fences, not entirely eager to go back to the silent house. There was always the mountain of paperwork to tackle. She saw the police car parked and Wayne on her front porch, and her heart began to beat faster.

What now?

She dismounted and took Merry inside the barn, not anxious for more bad news. She took the saddle off, then the blanket. "I have to talk to someone. I'll brush you down in a bit." She led Merry to the pasture just beyond the barn and let her go.

She made her way up the front porch and saw her gun sitting on the wicker table. "I guess I forgot about it."

"They found it when they brought your horse back here. I thought I'd bring it back to you."

"I appreciate it, Wayne."

"Got a minute?"

She glanced at him and nodded. "Come on in. I'll make us some coffee."

"Sounds good. Your coffee is much better than the swill they have at the station. I try and try to get the "master" recipe changed but Ingrid refuses."

"She just doesn't like the mud you like. Why don't you get one of those fancy ones that make a cup at a time?"

Wayne smiled as he sat at the kitchen table. "I'd have to make my own."

"I knew there had to be a good reason." She put the coffee on and kept busy straightening the kitchen while it brewed. She was putting off whatever he had to say but she just couldn't help it. Finally, she filled two mugs, handed one to Wayne and put the other on the table in front of where she sat.

He took a sip and smiled. "Just the way I like it. Hear tell Luke is at the motel. You kick him out?"

"I had his things put out on the porch before he got home—before he got here yesterday."

"Wished I'd seen them. I would have just taken him back to town. Poor guy."

"Poor guy? Poor Luke? Wayne, he lied and it wasn't a little lie. It was a lie of epic proportion, and I can't let that slide and pretend I don't know about it."

"I can understand why you're upset, but he was just a boy when it happened, and—"

"He is a full grown man now, and he should have told me."

"Now you know why he left so long ago. It had nothing to do with you."

"Why would you think I thought that?"

"Oh, come on, Meg. You stripped yourself of all femininity and refused to look at another man. You've had many admirers over the last few years."

Glancing down at her black shirt, she remembered what Luke had said about her being colorless. She felt colorless, as if all of the light had gone out of her life. She was the absence of color. "I know you mean well and all, but this is between me and Luke."

"Are you ever going to talk to him again?" Wayne stared at her.

"I just don't know what we'd have to say to one another. Done means it's over."

Wayne nodded and downed the last of his coffee. "Thank you for the great coffee. And, Meg, if he comes around listen for a minute before you shut him off. He really was caught up in things that weren't his fault. It was Harry who tried to get the ball rolling to have the land dug up. He hired the contractor. The project came to a halt when it was revealed that Harry no longer owned the land. The next week, Owen told the contractor to go ahead. He told him it was in Luke's best interest to be able to have money for cattle. I'm going but just remember, Luke is the only good one in the bunch."

Meg walked him to the door and said a pleasant good bye but she felt anything but pleasant. Wayne probably thought his words would comfort her in a small way but they didn't. She closed the door and once again, the silence echoed at her, mocking her. She went into the office and began to tackle the paperwork.

She forgot to ask Wayne about the shooter. She wanted to know if it was anyone, she knew. She started to divide payables, receivables, payroll, investments, and tons of other papers into categories and swore one day she'd hire a bookkeeper. She was good at many things but this was not one of them. She'd rather be on her horse, riding the range and working the ranch. It was all on her shoulders now so she'd buck up and get on with it.

It wasn't until she was nearly finished her stomach rumbled. She glanced at the clock and sighed, most of the day was already gone. She hadn't been eating right but she hadn't been hungry. Now perhaps she could manage to get something down. As she walked into the kitchen, she spied a woman on her porch, sitting in one of the chairs. She frowned as she crossed over to the door and opened it. "May I help you?"

The brown-haired, brown-eyed beauty glanced up at her and smiled. "I knocked but no one answered."

"How long ago was that?"

The woman stood, displaying her pregnant body. "About an hour ago. I didn't mind it's really nice out here. David was right, it is a place fit for a king."

Meg wondered if she was a bit touched in the head. "I like it. You're a friend of David's?"

"Why yes, I'm Marla, his fiancée. He called me last week and told me to pack my things and drive here. I suppose he'll be home soon." Her smile was bright.

"I'm not sure why he'd invite you to live in my house. Why don't you come in and have something to drink?" She held the door open for Marla to pass through.

Marla headed toward the kitchen and looked around. "You must be Meg. David told me a lot about you. He often spoke about growing up here with you. I'm so sorry about your father. David took the news very hard as you probably know."

Gesturing to the chair, Meg invited her to take a seat. "What can I get for you? Coffee or water?"

Marla stroked her stomach. "Water would be great, thank you."

"Coming right up." Meg turned and gritted her teeth. *How dare David invite his pregnant girlfriend to come and live here?* She put ice in a glass and poured water into it. "Here you go."

"Thank you," Marla said as she took the offered glass.

"Did you have a long drive?"

"No, it was only two hours. I was hurt at first when he didn't come back to see me but now I can see a place this size needs a lot of time and work. I'm so glad he was able to come and take over for you." She took a sip of water and then put the glass on the table. "I can't wait to see him."

"If you'll excuse me I have a call to make. I'll be right back." Meg quickly headed back into the office, closed the door, and groaned. There was no way she was going to tell Marla the truth about David. No, but she knew who should. Grabbing the phone, she then called Luke.

Luke rubbed the back of his neck as he drove Wayne's pick up. It was nice of him to lend him the truck. David had never mentioned Marla to him. He wasn't sure what to say to her, but Meg had been adamant on the phone that he needed to be the one to tell her. Heck, if it got him into the same room as Meg, he was all for it.

No sooner had he parked the truck, then the door to the house opened and there stood Meg. Her smile said it all. It was her fake, *I'm going to kill you*, smile. Hey, he'd take it for now. He jumped out of the truck and lumbered up to the door giving her his best grin, but his smile faded as her eyes narrowed.

"Thanks for coming."

"Was there any doubt?" He hated the coldness of her stare. He edged past Meg and found himself face-to-face with a lovely girl sitting at the table. That must be David's –Whoa! Meg had mentioned a fiancée but she didn't mention she was about to give birth anytime. He took off his hat and placed it on the rack. "You must be, Marla."

Her smiled was stunning. "Yes, yes I am. I'm so happy to meet you. David speaks very highly of you and his sister of course." She glanced behind him toward Meg.

"It's very nice to meet you, too." He glanced back over his shoulder hoping to get some type of cue from Meg. She actually smirked at him. He helped himself to some coffee and sat across the table from Marla. "How long did you plan to visit?"

"Visit? We must have our wires crossed. David said we were going to live in the house. He said you two sold your shares of the ranch to him." Her words sounded stilted as though she sensed her words were not true. Her smile dimmed as she glanced from him to Meg.

"Where's your stuff?" He asked gently.

"We really didn't have much. A friend of David's is packing up the house and bringing the contents in a few days. I got a ride from a friend. My bag is all I have with me. Why do I get the feeling something isn't right?" Her hands shook slightly as she brushed her long hair behind her shoulder.

Meg sat down next to him. Maybe she was done watching him squirm. "A lot has happened in the last day or two—"

"He's dead?"

"No, no, nothing like that. He doesn't have claim to any of this land. It all belongs to Meg."

Marla slowly shook her head. "But surely, I mean you're family. Where is David?"

Meg reached across the wooden table and took one of Marla's hands in hers. "David is in jail. I don't know how to sugarcoat the whole situation. The whole thing has me thrown so off balance I don't even know which way is up anymore."

Marla pulled her hand away. "David is a good man. Why would he be in jail? How is that possible?" She stood up. "Please take me to see him." Her face turned pasty white.

Luke jumped up and quickly rounded the table until he was at Marla's side. "Come on, let's get you settled on the couch and I'll tell you all of it. You look like you're going to faint on me."

She accepted his help to the couch and didn't protest as he helped put her feet up and placed a quilt over her. "Meg, please join us." He held his breath waiting for her answer.

"Of course. Marla, is there anything I can get you?"

Marla didn't answer. It was as though she hadn't heard her.

Luke waited for Meg to take a seat, then he sat in the chair next to her. "Oh boy, where to start? David is in jail on conspiracy to murder charges. Meg and I never planned to sell our shares of the ranch to him. I don't even own a share. This land runs through Meg's veins and she's very skilled at running it. It seems as though my dad, Harry, never had any claim to the land at all."

"Murder? They have the wrong person. Besides David's father is Meg's father so he would have claim to half the land at least. Harry didn't get a big payday selling the land?"

He felt a tingling in the back of his neck. Something about Marla wasn't right. She seemed even more interested in the money than David had been.

"Everyone thought David was Owen's son. Meg, here, only just found out before her father passed. Turns out Harry lied all those years to get money from Owen. It's a very jumbled history."

"This is all rather shocking," Marla said, her voice full of doubt.

"It is," Meg commented gently. "I wish I knew what to say to you."

"What is there to say? Somehow, David has been swindled. He is the owner of this ranch. He promised me this house and everyone knows ranchers have tons of money."

Luke exchanged glances with Meg. "We're telling you the truth."

Meg stood. "Look around you. Do you see riches and luxury? This is a working ranch, and everyone on it has to work to earn their pay and their keep."

Marla glared at Meg. "Not the wife."

"Yes, the wife, and the daughter. I've been the foreman on this ranch for almost five years. It's been backbreaking work with long hot hours in the saddle. You do know how to ride, don't you?"

Luke bit back a smile. Meg was obviously trying to get rid of Marla. "I came here after a car accident, barely able to walk and Meg put a broom in my hand and insisted I earn my keep. With you, being pregnant and all, you could do all the cooking for the ranch. Then when you have the baby you can keep it near you as you cook."

Marla pulled out her cellphone. "I need you to come get me. No, David lied. There is no ranch he owns." She hung up. "I will wait on the porch if you don't mind."

Meg smiled. "Don't you want to visit David in jail?"

Marla pulled her shoulders back. "No, I think I'll tell the real father of my baby he's going to be a daddy."

He blinked and stared at her. What kind of woman had David gotten himself mixed up with? "Go ahead and wait on the porch."

They watched her walk out of the door.

"Luke, what the heck?"

"I don't know. David never mentioned her at all but she did answer a lot of questions. Now we know why David was so interested in money."

"Sometimes I think I'm going insane. My whole world has changed and not for the better. I guess if I keep my focus on the ranch, things will turn out."

Luke stood and reached out for her, but she stepped back, out of his reach. "I'm sorry, Meg. I don't want you to flinch every time you see me."

She studied the floor for a while before lifting her gaze to his. Her eyes held tears, and his heart twisted. "I can't process everything. It's all been too much. Your part in this whole thing was unknowing, but you didn't trust me enough to tell me."

"I tried to put it out of my mind and when the body was found and it wasn't David, I thought for sure I was going to go down for the murder. I was scared. Too scared of losing you and going to jail. We finally got to a good place in our relationship, and there was no way I was going to let you go."

A tear trailed down her face, and he had to keep himself from wiping it away. She didn't want or need him.

"I feel as though everyone I know has lied to me. My life is built upon lies."

"Not entirely. Your parents loved each other and they loved you. I love you. Those are the constants in your life. The land you ride every day is a constant." He sighed. "I am sorrier than you'll ever know about my role in all this. I was a frightened kid when I left five years ago but I returned as a man. A battered man, but I should have known better. I like to think I have integrity but I don't know anymore." He clasped his hands in front of him not knowing what to do or how to act.

"I know. My love for you hasn't wavered and it's so hard. I can't be around you right now. You can move back to the bunkhouse and work the mustangs." She offered a helpless shrug. "I can't offer anything more than that."

The sadness in her eyes and the hurt in her voice made him feel two inches high. "I'll wait until Marla's ride comes and then go get my stuff from the motel. Thank you for letting me keep my job."

She gave him a curt nod. "I have paperwork to finish up." Then she walked away from him and loneliness shrouded him.

Hours later, Meg swore under her breath. Her father had sure left a mess. She lifted both hands into the air and stretched. He had tried to get her to learn how to do the paperwork, but she was always too busy. Now she wished she'd taken the time. At least it was keeping her mind occupied. She shivered, remembering Luke's attempt to touch her earlier. He'd meant to comfort her, and her response surprised her. It had been instinctive.

She grabbed another mound of paperwork and started sorting it. An invoice for the construction company was there. The company that had dug up the first body. She froze when she saw the date. It was dated the day Luke came back. She shook her head. Everything was suspect to her now. Maybe her father planned on the condominiums before Luke came back. There could be many reasons, couldn't there?

Leaning back in the leather chair, she closed her eyes. "Breathe, just breathe," she repeated until heart stopped banging against her ribs. Finally, she relaxed a bit and leaned forward planting her elbows on the desk. Just as she started to lower her face against her hands, she caught sight of the invoice again.

Picking up the phone, she called Ray, the man who wanted to develop the land. He answered the phone and they exchanged greetings. When she asked about the property, he hesitated.

"It was a bit strange," he said. I was surprised your dad would want to part with his land, but he said he wanted to see what it was worth. I've been after him for years to sell me some of your prime land."

"You scheduled it for weeks later?"

It was the earliest date I would be free."

"It's strange don't you think? Why would Harry call you?"

Ray paused. "I have my suspicions but they're only my thoughts. I think Harry knew there were bodies on the property and wanted your father to go down for them."

Her stomach dropped. "I think you may be right, Ray. Thanks for answering my questions. I appreciate it."

"Anytime, Meg. Take care." He hung up the phone

Exhausted, she needed coffee. On her way to the kitchen, she was startled to see Luke still in the house. "What are you doing here?"

"Before you get mad, I just wanted to be sure you wanted me to work for you. I don't want to take a handout."

"You're good with the mustangs. My time on horseback is getting limited with all the rest of the ranch work. It'll be fine."

He tipped his hat and gave her a half smile. "Just wanted to be sure. I'll see you around."

She watched him walk away, remembering what his hands felt like on her body. He was so sexy in his Wranglers. If only things were different. Just when she thought her heart was broken completely, the last of it shattered. A colorless life was a safer life. A much safer life, no more heartbreaks this big. She loved the land, the animals, and the men who worked for her. It was going to be harder than she thought having Luke on her property. *Damn, he lost all of his dreams too.*

There would be no house built together, no ranch to start. It must have been a huge blow to him, losing his ranch, and finding out his brother and father were monsters. Poor Luke, they'd both been piled on with manure. Her father did want him to have the land. She'd have to think about it. A bit of distance between them was good, maybe she could think it all out logically.

She began to pace in the front room, trying to think. Her father really did plan to give Luke and David the land even after Harry called Ray. Harry tried to set him up and thank goodness, he stopped it. David was out of the equation of course. That left Luke. What would Luke's fate be?

It had been a week since Luke had moved back into the bunkhouse, and he'd never been more miserable. He'd thought perhaps Meg seeing him every day would soften her up some. It was not the case. She avoided him and ignored him. The smallest glimpse made his heart beat faster and a rush of failure went through his veins. He'd been so close to his dreams and now he was- hell he didn't even know where he was.

Perhaps he was a constant reminder to her of the pain and misery she'd endured. He asked around trying to find a new job, one that was close but no one would hire him. The name Kelly was forever equated with Mud.

Standing in the shade of the bunkhouse roof, he watched Meg hurry out of the house and run toward the barn. Greg exited with both Merry and another horse, both saddled. He took a giant step into the sunlight. It looked serious.

Meg saw him. "I'm going to need your help. One of the mustangs is down, and we need to figure out why."

Luke nodded. "I'm right behind you."

Meg and Greg rode out leaving a cloud of dust behind them. He started toward the barn trying to walk as fast as possible. He damned his injuries and saddled up the blue roan. Which horse was it?

He rode out and was soon just behind Meg and Greg. At least Greg had his rifle with him, in case… Luke's chest tightened. He should have thought to bring his rifle. If the horse was suffering, they'd have to put it down. The horses had been his solace the last few days.

Finally, the downed mustang was in sight. His throat felt raw as he recognized the horse, it was Damia, a young filly. Before he could reach her, a shot rang out. Greg had put her down. Luke's horse grew skittish but he soon had him in hand. He rode up next to Merry and got off his horse.

Meg's head was bowed, and Greg talked quietly to her. She nodded a time or two. Clearly out of his element as he shifted his weight from one foot to another, he nodded at Luke.

"I wish there was something I could have done."

"We all go through it, Greg," Luke reassured him.

Meg stared at him, her eyes wide. "It was Damia." Her shaky breath warned him of the tears to come.

Greg took a step back. "I'll head to the house and get a few men out here."

"I'll stay with, Meg."

Greg nodded and shuffled away. He got on his horse, tipped his hat to them, and was off.

"She had potential. Don't you think Luke?" Tears flowed down her face.

"She did at that. One of the best."

"Luke?"

"Yes?"

"Why are all these bad things happening to me? Am I cursed? Did I do something horrible? I don't think I can take much more." Her pink lips trembled as she spoke.

He opened his arms and was relieved when she stepped into the circle of them. Pulling her close he felt each sob against him. She had a lot to be sad about. Some of it was his own doing. Placing his chin on top of her head, he stroked her back, trying to think of what to say.

She clung to him tightly, and he wished he could take her pain away. Losing Damia was the last straw, he supposed. He rocked her back and forth as her sobs lessoned. He breathed in her scent, all horses and hay, knowing it would be the last time she'd let him hold her. A lump formed in his throat. He loved her with all his heart and he'd lost her.

"Do you think?" She stepped away from him. "Did Greg—"

"Greg did the right thing, sweetheart. Look at her leg. She must have been running wild and free to have it break like that. It's a shame."

"I haven't seen you much lately." She kept her gaze just right of him.

"I've been earning my keep." He shrugged as a smile tugged at his mouth. "Happily earning my keep. These horses are good for what ails my heart. Well at least somewhat. They take up much of my time and I don't have too much down time to think."

"What do you think about?"

He wasn't sure what the right answer would be, so he simply told her the truth. "I think about you. I think about what we could have had. Mostly I think about how I lost you. It's not an easy thing. I've been trying to find work elsewhere so you wouldn't have to see me around but no one is hiring. I think about the way you smell and how your lips taste. I relive making love to you and seeing your smile."

There was no expression on her face and she didn't even glance at him. He'd given it one last try and now he knew for certain. They weren't meant to be. A part of him died inside as he turned toward his horse. Taking a deep breath, he braced himself, slowly let the breath out and then asked, "Do you want me to wait for you or go on?"

"Go on."

He mounted the roan and rode off. Her words were forever words. She didn't want him and she never would. He'd widen his scope for a new job. There was no reason to stay close, it was too painful. With his leg, he wasn't sure if anyone would take him on, but it was time to go forward and find his future. He recognized the pain rolling through him. It was grief.

Luke's Fate

Kathleen Ball

Chapter Eight

One week later, Meg woke before the sun and made herself get up. The urge to stay in bed had been with her all week. *One foot in front of the other* was her constant litany. Dragging herself out of bed, made each of her muscles ache but she quickly got dressed. Now every time she put on a shirt she muttered "colorless." Things had to get better.

The phone rang and she answered it. "Meg, it's Greg. Luke's gone."

"What do you mean he's gone?"

"He packed up and left."

"Where did he go?"

"I don't know. There isn't a note and he never said anything about leaving."

"Thanks for letting me know."

She slid onto a chair and hung up the phone then sat very quietly, not moving an inch. Luke had left the night before. He hadn't even said good-bye. Life was not supposed to hurt like this. The anguish she felt was crippling. This time the land would not bring her joy.

Sighing heavily, she stood and walked outside. She had work to do. In the barn, she grabbed the bridle and saddle and got Merry ready. It was time to let go, and that meant selling the mustangs.

The morning breeze was pleasant as she rode out. There was plenty of nature to admire on her way, but her eyes were unseeing. The mustangs were her last link to Luke and as much as it hurt, it was best to cut all ties. Luke had given her a list of buyers before the canyon shooting. She'd probably get a good price for them. They would have given Luke enough money to live wherever he wanted. She'd gotten his message loud and clear by his leaving without telling her.

She watched them frolic and a brief smile graced her lips. She'd been watching over the herd for quite some time now. Each horse had his or her own personalities. They were much like people. Some were mischievous and some more focused. Some were very intelligent and a few, well they weren't so bright, but she loved them all.

With them gone, she wouldn't have much reason to come onto this part of the land. They'd use the land for grazing but that wasn't her job anymore. She was the owner, not the foreman. Giving the herd one more appraising look, she then turned Merry and rode for home. She had a few phone calls to make.

She was pleased when she got home and looked the list over. She'd heard of at least half of them. It was obvious Luke wanted the horses to go to good places. How long would it take her to forget him? Maybe it was asking too much. How long would it take her to not want to break down and cry? She needed to work on that first but the pain in her heart told her it would be a long time coming.

The decision was made, and she'd might as well begin making phone calls. She called Rudy Price first. He had a big horse ranch, and she respected him. He sounded like a little boy at Christmas who received a gift he'd been waiting for. He made her promise not to call anyone else and he'd be out in a few days. What else could she do? She promised.

It didn't make her feel one lick better. In fact, she felt guilty about selling the mustangs. She kept reminding herself Luke had left. She went into the kitchen and sat at the table. The house was so very quiet. The refrigerator hummed occasionally but beyond that, there was silence. The kitchen table seemed bigger than before. If only her dad was still alive.

She longed to go to the bunkhouse and hang out but that wasn't the way of things. She was the owner not a cowhand. She'd been so busy trying to be a rough and tough foreman; she hadn't made time for friends. Some were married, she supposed, with kids. A giant lump grew in her throat and she swallowed hard against it. She'd survive. Happiness was never a promise but a desire. In her case, it was a dream that had died.

She stood and shook her head. Her father wouldn't want her to wallow in pity. The O'Briens were made of hearty stock. Maybe if she started networking with the local ranch owners, she'd find peers she could call friends. Feeling better for having some type of plan she went to bed.

By rights, she should move into her dad's room. It was much larger, a better fit for the ranch's owner, but she couldn't bring herself to do it yet. Time would be the key for her. She needed to give it time. As she lay in bed, she heard the wind kicking up and rain began to pelt down. She jumped out of bed and drew on her robe. Just as she thought, it was hail, the size of a golf ball hitting and bouncing everywhere. She hoped the stock would be okay.

There weren't that many places for them to go to get out of the bad weather.

The hail drummed hard on the roof as lightening etched across the sky. Thunder boomed, and the house shook. It wasn't like her to have bad weather sneak up on her. Checking the weather was a duty she'd neglected. Mistakes could take a life out here. From now on, she planned to be on her game.

This time, she was determined to pull herself together. There was no other choice if she wanted everyone to be safe. She had a job to do and by golly, she was going to get it done. No more insipid hurt feelings for her.

Now if only her heart would agree.

Rudy had been called out of town for over a week, and finally he was coming to see the mustangs. Meg had mixed feelings about selling them. She'd cared for them and trained them. It was just something she had to do for her own sanity.

Words of strength were good but her heart still ached. She had ridden more than usual, trying to tire her body out for a good night's sleep. It felt wonderful to ride out each day to check on the cattle, the fences and of course the horses. She'd even attended one of the local meetings the ranchers had. It was informative and she did shake many hands but none she could consider friends yet.

She grabbed orange juice out of the refrigerator and poured herself a glass. Rudy was running late. Greg was on look out for him. He would have a few horses ready for them. He was a good, dependable guy.

Finally, just as she finished her juice a shiny red pick-up drove in. It was pretty flashy. She always bought practical trucks. She checked herself in the mirror and frowned at the navy blue t-shirt she wore. She shrugged her shoulders. It was practical too

Putting a spring in her step and a smile on her face, she bounded out the door ready to greet Rudy. Only it wasn't Rudy who got out of the truck. It was Luke. She gasped and her smile faded. "Working for the Price's?"

"In a roundabout way," he answered staring at her.

"What does that mean?" She put her hands on her hip and narrowed her eyes.

"It means Rudy wants me to check the horses and make an offer." His stare made her uncomfortable.

"I wondered where you went."

"Aw, Meg, it was easier for both of us if I didn't say goodbye. My heart wouldn't have been able to survive."

Her hands dropped to her sides. "I suppose you're right. Let's go check out the horses. I'm surprised Rudy didn't come himself."

"He trusts me."

Three little words and they jabbed at her conscience. She walked to the barn and took Merry's reins from Greg. "Thanks."

"Are you going to be okay? I can easily saddle up another horse and ride with you."

Giving him a sad smile, she shook her head. "I appreciate the offer but this is something I need to do myself."

Greg nodded and gave Luke a dirty look as he handed him the reins to the grey roan.

They both mounted and were off. She glanced at him often as they rode toward the herd. She caught him glancing at her too. They didn't speak. She didn't know what to say. Her heart beat a loud tattoo and she was certain he could hear it. They pulled up as soon as the mustangs were in sight.

"Magnificent aren't they?" Luke asked.

"They sure are. I'm glad you will still be a part of them." She stared at the horses at play.

"Are you?"

"Hmm?"

"Are you glad I'll have the mustangs?"

Turning her head, she gazed at him. His eyes were filled with love and pain. She wanted to tell him it all didn't matter and she loved him, but...

"Yes, I am glad. They know you."

The little hope he'd had in his expression quickly faded. "Yes, I thought it a good decision. I'm surprised you wanted to sell all of them."

"You know, a clean break and all. It's best for everyone."

"Oh, Meg, you don't mean it. I can see into your heart, and you don't want this. I know you love me." The pleading in his voice almost made her give up her resolve.

"I do want this. It's for the best."

"You keep saying it's for the best, but how? Explain how being apart is for the best. Have you been happy the last few weeks? Are you sleeping?"

Slowly she got off Merry, not knowing what to say. She didn't know how it was the best. "I just need to forget you, and the mustangs are too much of a reminder of how stupid I was to wait five years for you and then fall into your arms as soon as you came back."

Luke dismounted. "Sweetheart you most certainly did not fall into my arms. It was a hard fight, and I'd gladly fight for you again. I know I hurt you, and I'm so sorry. I wish I was never there that night, and I wish I had been brave enough to stand up to my father. I was weak."

"No, Luke, you weren't weak. Your father was evil, plain and simple. You knew he'd have hurt you if you hadn't helped him."

"Maybe." Luke rubbed the back of his neck. "I should have told someone, but I turned and ran all for nothing."

She reached out and touched his arm. "Not for nothing. You had a wife and a beautiful girl and they needed you. I admit I was hurt when I found out you had married, but I came to admire what you did." His arm grew warm to her touch.

"About the horses. What kind of price are we talking about?" He asked as he took a step away from her.

"The same as we discussed before all this happened." He was physically and emotionally distancing himself from her.

"No family discount?" He looked as though he wanted to take his words back.

She smiled sadly. "We're not family."

"Then what are we?" His eyes hardened.

"We're not anything." To her mortification, tears rolled down her face. "Apart we are good, just not together."

"So, that's it? It's all black and white to you? I didn't tell you about my role in this big mess and I'm no longer a man to be trusted?"

Leaving Merry behind, she walked closer to the mustangs. It was going to be very hard to sell them. It was a good thing Luke could take them. They would be well cared for and she'd never see him again." Her heart ached beyond anything she'd felt before. Everything else Luke had done proved he was a man of integrity. He was a hardworking, loving man, and he loved her.

"We'll take them all," Luke said when he finally caught up to her.

"I've decided not to sell."

"Seriously? Damn it, Meg, Make up your mind."

She gazed into his eyes. "I have made up my mind. I want the mustangs. And I want you."

His eyes flickered in surprise. "As what? You want me as what?"

"Luke I want you as the man in my life. I want you as the one I love unconditionally. I also need you to train the mustangs." She smiled.

"I'm up for the mustangs but the rest, I don't know." His grin was deep and it filled her heart.

"As long as I don't have to let you go."

"Sweetheart, I'm not going anywhere. I want us to get married and have a family and work together. It's all I ever wanted." He closed the distance between them and lifted her up for a kiss. He swung her around with his arms holding her tight.

"Put me down!"

"Yes, ma'am." He gently set her on her feet. "I love you."

"I love you too, Luke."

Luke's Fate

Thank you for reading **_Luke's Fate_** by Award Winning, Amazon Best-Selling Author Kathleen Ball! If you'd like to read more of Kathleen Ball's books you can find them here: <u>Amazon</u>

And you can find her here on Facebook

<u>https://www.facebook.com/kathleenballwesternromance/</u>

Made in the USA
San Bernardino, CA
05 August 2016